Could, or would, he ever let himself fall in love?

Michael had thought about <del>S0-BEA-256</del> ever did. He'd thought about what kind would be attracted to someone like him.

Of course he'd be lying to himself if he said his injury didn't bother him. That it wasn't the reason he'd avoided any number of women who'd made advances on him these past months since he'd come to work as the ship's doctor. God knows, he wasn't a saint when it came to that part of his life. Yet right now, getting involved in *any* manner wasn't right, not when he had so little to offer someone else.

But Sarah…she was different. She was someone who intrigued him. Someone who captured his interest and held it. Someone so sexy and yet so vulnerable he couldn't even begin to imagine what it would be like to have a woman like that in his life for a little while, or maybe even forever. He hadn't meant to look, hadn't meant to go any further after he had looked. Sarah was on his mind in ways he didn't want and couldn't control.

Dear Reader,

When I first started thinking about where I wanted to set my story *The Wife He's Been Waiting For,* we were having a long, gloomy wet snap at home. The weather was dreary, ugly and cold. I wanted to escape and go somewhere sunny and warm, but I couldn't right then. So I did the next best thing. I set my story in the area that would have been my perfect escape—on a cruise ship in the Caribbean. Even if I couldn't go there in person, my mind traveled there every day for all the weeks I was writing my book.

Some people might call that strange, but for me, books have always been my portal to the world. Pick up one book and see what's hidden within the pages and you'll be surprised where you might go.

When I was younger, Harlequin became my window to the world at least a couple of times a month as I searched out new books to read. It's still my window to the world, only now it allows me to take you with me wherever I go. So next time it's dreary, ugly and cold outside, stay inside, curl up in bed or in your favorite chair next to the fireplace, pick up a book and have yourself a wonderful journey!

Wishing you health, happiness and pleasant destinations!

Dianne Drake

P.S. It's always so nice hearing from my readers, and I appreciate your e-mails! As always, you can contact me at Dianne@DianneDrake.com.

THE WIFE HE'S BEEN WAITING FOR
Dianne Drake

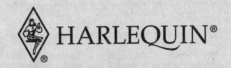

TORONTO • NEW YORK • LONDON
AMSTERDAM • PARIS • SYDNEY • HAMBURG
STOCKHOLM • ATHENS • TOKYO • MILAN • MADRID
PRAGUE • WARSAW • BUDAPEST • AUCKLAND

Recycling programs
for this product may
not exist in your area.

ISBN-13: 978-0-373-06677-3
ISBN-10:   0-373-06677-5

THE WIFE HE'S BEEN WAITING FOR

First North American Publication 2009

THE WIFE HE'S BEEN WAITING FOR

With all my heart, I dedicate this book to Jason, and all the brave ones in the battlefield, wherever it may be.

CHAPTER ONE

THE sound of laughter wafted though the walls of Sarah's cabin. People in the hallways were anxious to get underway, were planning the holiday of their lives, with expectations of fun and adventure on this cruise. Not only expectations, but so many dreams were invested in a few simple days. They would eat all the marvelous foods fixed by the gourmet chefs on board. See new sights they'd only seen in picture books. Make new friends. Visit the various ports and come away with gifts and mementoes of the wonderful time they'd had on this cruise—things they wouldn't think of buying back home—like hideously large straw hats and brightly colored plastic gecko lizards. Memories to last a lifetime.

But for Dr Sarah Collins, none of that was going to happen. Staring out the porthole, she sighed the same sad sigh she'd been sighing for months now. It never changed, no matter where she went or what she did. It simply never changed.

Continuing with the task of tucking her clothes into the closet and tiny bureau, she wondered about taking part in some of the shipboard activities, then immediately wiped that out of her mind. Sure, it was a holiday, just like the last one had been and the one before that. Thanks to a conservative lifestyle while she had been a practicing doctor, and a lucrative sale of her part of the medical practice after she'd decided not to practice medicine any longer, her life had been a succession of holidays this past year, skipping, without thought or too much planning, from one to another, like she hadn't a care in the world.

Quite the contrary was true, though. That's all she had—cares, memories, sadness. Which was why her life had turned into a series of events requiring no commitment. What better way to avoid reality than by going on holiday? Over and over again.

This was her first cruise, though, and she wasn't sure why she'd chosen it. It was so…populated. Hundreds and hundreds of people. Planned activities. Normally, she stuck to herself. A self-guided foot tour of Paris was perfect as no one paid any attention to a single woman passing her days wandering the streets, tourist sights, museums, and her nights tucked into a cabaret corner, spending all evening nursing one or two glasses of wine, listening to the cabaret singer spill out her own version of the blues. In those moments she felt a connection to the singer, understanding how life had a way of slapping you down the way the singer was depicting in her words. But all too soon the night and the music would end and Sarah was on to the next day, next destination. A rental car to see the castles of Scotland, where no one took a second look at a solitary tourist passing though. A hike through the Canadian Rockies and bicycling up the coast of Nova Scotia. Both very nice, and quite solitary.

Then this. To be honest, she couldn't explain what had gotten into her, booking a cruise. Two weeks long at that. Maybe it was the boredom factor finally creeping in, or her lack of companionship these last months. Normally she was a very social person, loved being around other people. Maybe that's what was getting to her—the isolation. Or maybe she'd just run out of ideas and this had seemed easy.

Whatever the case, she was here, in a tiny little cabin with sparse amenities, not sure about her decision. For her to find all the amenities a cruise offered, she'd have to leave her cabin and mingle with the other passengers, and while that did seem appealing, it was also more frightening than anything she'd taken on in the past year.

Just thinking about what she was about to embark on caused Sarah's hands to shake, made her break out in a cold sweat.

Damn, it was happening again.

The walls were closing in on her. The ceiling inching down. Room spinning.

Deep breath, Sarah. You know what it is.

Gripping the edge of the bureau, she hung on praying for the feeling to pass. This had been a stupid, crazy idea! Even entertaining the notion that she could endure two weeks on a ship was totally insane. Yet here she was, getting ready to set sail, and having another panic attack over it.

Breathe, Sarah. One more deep breath and you'll be fine.

Two weeks of this, either cooped up and alone or mixing with so many people that even the thought of it nauseated her.

Another breath. You can do this.

It hit her all of a sudden. Once they set sail she couldn't get off. Bad thought. Wrong thought. Her pulse was racing now, her breaths so shallow her lips were tingling.

"Got to get off." The urge to run was hitting her so hard and violently it nearly choked the breath out of her. She had to get off. Now! Couldn't wait. Forget the clothes, they were only clothes. They could be replaced.

Sarah bolted for the door, fumbled the latch with shaking hands, then finally threw it open, looked first to the left, then to the right to get her bearings. Elevator…to the right, she thought. She had to get there. There was still time. Had to be enough time. She hadn't heard the all-ashore warning, had she?

Running hard, zigging and zagging in and out of the other passengers on their way to locate cabins, she did make it to the elevator and managed to squeeze in just as the doors were about to shut. "Excuse me," she gasped, wedging her way between a buxom older lady smelling of gardenias and wearing a large purple hat that took up enough space for two people and a hard body in a white uniform she didn't care to investigate. "Could I just have a little more room?"

Too many people crammed in, too many different cloying perfumes, too many voices... "More room, please," she begged again, just as the elevator started to spin. Not literally. She knew that. It was her head spinning. Damn, she'd meant to eat something this morning...last night.

Stupid! She was a doctor. She knew better. But she recognized a good case of low blood sugar when she felt it, and she felt it. *As soon as I get off the ship*, she promised herself. She'd go and find the closest little café to the dock and have herself a decent meal. Except the claustrophobia left over from her panic attack combined with the wooziness of her hypoglycemia were conspiring to bring her to her knees. As the elevator dinged its way from deck to deck, without anyone getting off, she was glad for the crowded conditions now as there was no way she could make it to her knees.

But her body was trying to make her collapse. Voices getting louder...smells stronger...ringing in her ears. Head spinning...no place to fall except into the immense bosom of the purple hat lady or into the hard body behind her.

In the end, the decision wasn't Sarah's to make. As the elevator jolted to a stop on yet another deck, her head took its last spin and she sank directly into the arms of the hard body, who had the good sense to hold her up until everybody was off the elevator. Then he scooped her up into his arms and carried her out.

She was vaguely aware of him, vaguely aware that she was babbling something incoherent. She knew that she wanted to get off the ship and go someplace where she could be alone again. But all the vagueness lasted mere seconds, then nothing. Sarah had passed out in the arms of a stranger.

"Everybody, out at the next stop," Dr Michael Sloan ordered, as the dark-haired woman slumped against his chest. She wasn't unconscious yet, but he'd bet his medical license that would be the next thing to happen.

He'd noticed her when she'd got on. Pale, nervous. Panicked look on her face. Or maybe frightened. Whichever it was, she'd squeezed in and the instant the doors had shut he'd noticed her breathing. Shallow, rapid. All indicators of someone who didn't want to be there. Panic attack, maybe. Or someone in some kind of real physical distress. Then she'd gone and slumped into him, right into his arms, like she'd had it planned, and now the only thing he could do was hold onto her until they could get off. Then he'd take a look, see what the problem was.

As the doors parted, the dozen or so people crammed into the elevator started to file out while he kept a tight hold on his new patient. He'd never before had one drop into his arms the way this one had. In fact, he couldn't recall that he'd ever had any woman swoon like this, whether or not she had been sick. Too bad this one was sick, because he liked the way she smelled. Fresh, something fruity, he thought as the last three people left, leaving him enough room to lead her through the doors.

Yes, he definitely liked her scent. It wasn't the heavy, sickly sweet scent of expensive perfume he smelled so often on the ship. Turning in the direction of the doors, he prepared to exit. "Now, somebody, please hold the door open for me."

The woman with the monster purple hat wedged her ample body in the door opening to prevent it from closing as Michael started to assist his patient through the elevator doors, but after two steps her full weight sagged against him and he had no other recourse but to pick her up and carry her out.

"Get off," she mumbled at him. "Want off…now. Have to…off…"

"We are. Right now," he replied. "We're getting off right now."

"Got to go… Can't stay…"

"That's right. We're going to my office," he replied, as she tucked her head against his chest. "I'm the ship's doctor and I think I need to have a little look at you to see what's going on."

"Want to go…please, let me…"

"Don't worry. I'll get you back to your cabin once I've given you an exam," he said, already deciding she might be in the throes of hypoglycemia. That happened a lot. People got excited about the cruise, then forgot to eat. The next thing that happened was their blood sugar whacking out. It wasn't uncommon and usually very easy to fix. "When was the last time you ate something? Do you remember?" She looked particularly frail, he thought, and a good several pounds under her ideal weight. Pretty, though. Add another ten pounds and she'd be voluptuous. For a moment he envisioned her looking vibrant—her face with some color in it to better contrast with the raven black of her hair, her dark brown eyes filled with something other than anguish. The more he studied her, the more he was taken by her beauty.

Then she shifted in his arms, laid her hand on his chest and for an instant he felt a tingle, which immediately snapped his attention back to his professional assessment of her. Without a test, hypoglycemia was still his first call. That's what he had to keep his mind on, that he was carrying a patient to his office, not a beautiful woman to his bed.

Although it had been a long time since he'd had a woman there, no matter how she got there—walking on her own, carried in his arms, or somersaulting.

"Too loud. So many people…" she mumbled, snapping him back once again. "Don't want to—"

"Can you tell me if you have low blood sugar?" he interrupted, his voice rather stiff and husky. "Have you ever been diagnosed with a condition called hypoglycemia?"

Instead of answering, she merely sighed, then snuggled in a little more. And snaked her arm up around his neck, causing another tingle to skitter off the tips of her fingers and run down the full length of his back.

Michael cleared his throat heavily, like that would clear away the tingle. "Have you been diagnosed with…" He tried again, but her other arm went up, and now what should have been a simple hold on a patient looked more like a lover's embrace. But only for a moment, then both her arms went limp and her hold on him vanished.

His patient had fainted again.

Sarah finally opened her eyes, squinting into the overhead exam light, before she twisted her head to the side and opened them fully. Where was she? Why was she here? "What's that?" she asked, spotting the IV stand with its bag hanging next to the bed, not yet realizing that it was anchored into her arm.

"Sugar water," came a voice from the other side of a blue-and-green-striped curtain. "Your blood sugar was low so we're giving you something to bring it back up to normal."

Curtain, hard bed… She glanced around as the surroundings started making sense to her. Medical equipment. Now it was all coming back. Panic attack, hypoglycemic episode. She'd gotten into the elevator. It had been crowded…she did remember that much. The perfume, the large woman with the purple hat. Then she'd keeled over, hadn't she?

An involuntary moan slipped through Sarah's lips as her recall returned in full and she remembered collapsing straight into the hard body's arms. Now here she was in the ship's hospital. As a patient, though. Not as a doctor.

"We did a little test," he continued.

Well, of course he would, she thought, not too surprised by his verdict. This was the hospital and he was a medic of some sort. "How low was it? My blood sugar?"

"Forty-two when I brought you in. Normal values start at eighty, and run all the way up to one-twenty. But you were well under the norm, which was why you passed out."

She knew all that. Her days as a practicing physician might be over, but her medical knowledge was certainly as good as ever. It had been only a little over a year since she'd quit medicine altogether, and yet she still read the journals to keep up, even though she had no intention of returning to practice again. But old habits died hard, and her love of medicine hadn't diminished one bit.

Naturally, she wasn't going to explain all that to the medic. No need to. As far as he was concerned, she was merely another tourist on holiday who'd gone and done something stupid, like forgetting to eat. And, actually, that's what she was, wasn't it? The perpetual tourist? "I don't suppose I've eaten anything for a while," she admitted, almost too embarrassed to say so since she did know better.

"How long ago?" he asked.

He had a nice voice. Soothing. Deep. The kind of voice a patient would trust. "Two or three meals, I think," she stated, although she was pretty sure she'd skipped maybe one more than that. "I was…uh…excited about the cruise. All the arrangements, last-minute details." Such a lie. Over this past year she'd neglected to eat as many meals as she'd eaten. Truth was, she had no appetite. She would eat occasionally, but only enough to sustain her, to keep her blood-sugar levels intact. Except this time she hadn't even done that much, and she was mildly embarrassed for messing up that way. "As soon as the dextro…um, the sugar water is in, can I get off the ship?"

"I'm afraid you were still pretty groggy when the ship set sail half an hour ago. Which means you're on a cruise now."

Michael stepped out from behind the curtain, stopping at the foot of the bed. "And from the looks of things, you could probably use the rest."

Handsome man, she thought. Strikingly so. Tall, a little over six feet, broad shoulders, athletic build. Dark brown hair, with eyes to match. Nice smile. But his eyes were…well, she couldn't tell. They weren't unfriendly, but they didn't sparkle. "Believe me, I've had plenty of rest." That was an understatement. She'd had nothing but rest since she'd quit her medical practice.

"You were trying to get off the ship, weren't you? That's why you were so frantic in the elevator. You weren't going to stay and take the cruise."

"I changed my mind. Decided I didn't want to…" That sounded like a silly explanation, didn't it? She'd spent thousands of dollars to book a two-week cruise, then changed her mind minutes before setting sail. It sounded silly enough that he probably thought her addle-brained.

"It could have been the hypoglycemia talking. The lower your blood sugar gets, the more that can alter your thinking. Once you've rested up, got a good meal in you, and your blood sugar is staying normal and not fluctuating, you'll change your mind and start enjoying all the things we have to offer here."

"Not necessary. I'll be fine, um… I didn't catch your name."

"Sloan," he said. "Michael Sloan." He walked around the bed, extending a hand to her. "In case you're wondering, I'm the one you collapsed onto in the elevator."

She'd already guessed as much. Somehow she had recognized the hard body, even though this was the first time she'd seen his face. An amazing face. "I'm Sarah Collins," she said, taking his hand. Nice, soft. Good touch for a doctor…for anybody. "Like I was saying, it's not necessary for me to stay here and take up your time or your hospital space. I'm fine now. Ready to have the IV out so I can go back to my cabin, since it seems I'm taking a cruise. Or, at least, the first leg of it."

"Well, my hospital space is your hospital space. You're my first patient of the cruise and I think I'd like to hang onto you a little while longer just to show the ship's captain that I'm earning my keep." He chuckled. "And by the time we've reached the first port you might decide that taking a cruise isn't such a bad idea.'

It wasn't such a good idea either. "Well, you weren't the one who started your cruise with such a bang the way I did, were you?" she said, her voice sagging into disappointment. It really didn't make any difference where she was—on a cruise in the Caribbean, on a camel somewhere in Egypt, in a cyclo in Cambodia. It had all been the same lately. One place after another, and she'd hardly noticed any of it. "But thank you for doing the gallant thing and bringing me to the hospital. I suppose if I had to collapse into somebody's arms, it was a good thing I chose a doctor's."

"It was either me or the lady in the purple hat."

He smiled at her and his eyes flickered into a genuinely little sparkle. Not much, but it was there. Nice eyes, she thought. Nice sparkle, too, although very short-lived. Come and gone in an instant. "So what's your best guess on how long I'll be here?" she asked.

"I want to do another blood test in about ten minutes, then we'll see."

"Have you done a blood test since the initial one?" she asked, trying not to sound so clinical. What concerned her was that a reading of forty-two wasn't too far from critical or even near-death in some cases. She recalled a patient at her clinic not all that long ago who'd gone into cardiac arrest at a blood sugar of thirty-five, and couldn't be revived. Just another reason to quit medicine, she rationalized. Things that should be easily reversed weren't always what they seemed. One small speck of melanoma should have been easy to remove, easy to treat. A little case of being overtired should have been cured by a couple days of rest.

But what should have been didn't always happen. Or, in her case, didn't ever happen.

"Your blood sugar's seventy now. Good, but not good enough to be up and wandering around yet."

"Then how about I go back to my cabin right now, go to bed and order something sweet from room service?" That was the easy way to do it, then she didn't have to be bothered by anyone, including the doctor.

"How about you stay right where you are for another ten minutes, then we'll decide what you'll get to do after that?"

That worked too, she supposed. It wasn't like she had someplace else to go, or anything else to do. And she really did want to prove that old saying wrong, that doctors made the worst patients. It wasn't her aim to be a bad patient. Dr Sloan was only doing his job and she didn't want to give him any grief over it. In other words, she wanted to be the kind of patient she used to like treating, so she'd stay there and take his advice. "Ten minutes," she agreed, then shut her eyes, not so much to sleep as to simply block him out. This past year she'd stayed away from a lot of things—life, commitments, friends—and the one thing she'd assiduously avoided at all costs had been anything medical. Dr Michael Sloan, handsome as he was, standing there with his stethoscope around his neck and a chart in his hand, was definitely medical. And definitely someone to avoid.

Too bad. Something else on her list of things to avoid was becoming involved in another relationship. Two so far, and all she'd done had been to prove what a miserable failure she was. She'd had two wonderful men in her life and the best she'd done in both relationships had been to fail them. Miserably.

So what was the point of even looking, when that's as far

as she'd let it go? Honestly, buying one of those brightly colored plastic gecko lizards the tourists all seemed so thrilled over didn't seem like such a bad idea for a relationship. At least she wouldn't let a chunk of red, yellow and green plastic down.

Or kill it.

Well, she wasn't sleeping. Trying hard to pretend she was, perhaps, but he knew better. In spite of her attempt to even out her breathing, her eyelids were fluttering—a dead giveaway that she was awake and faking sleep.

Michael chuckled as he returned to his office. Something big was bothering her, but he wasn't going to guess what it was. Wasn't even going to pry. He was a doctor whose commitment to his patients was only as long as this two-week cruise. He took care of their physical woes while they were on the ship, then said goodbye to them as he welcomed aboard a new bunch. That's all he was here for—to treat them and leave them—which suited him just fine. So if there was something about Sarah Collins that needed figuring out other than a case of hypoglycemia, he'd leave that puzzle to someone else. Lord knew, he was the last one to figure out anybody...especially himself.

"Repeat a finger-stick in about five minutes," he instructed Ina Edwards, one of the ship's nurses. "And let me know what it is."

"You OK, Mike?" she asked him. "Your leg? Can I get you something?"

Old enough to be his mother, Ina doted on him. And while she meant well, and he appreciated the concern, it annoyed him. He was fine. Perfect. Just dandy. Except people didn't want to believe that. One war injury and a couple of years later so many pieces of his broken world still weren't back in place. But he didn't take it out on those who cared about him. He merely smiled his way through it. People cared. They wanted to show compassion he didn't deserve, though, considering what he'd done.

Sighing, Michael faked a smile at Ina. "I'm fine, thanks. Just not prepared to start duty so early into the cruise. Normally they don't start coming in until after the first round of bon-voyage parties. Hangovers and all that."

"Well, I can go fix you a cup of tea," she offered, not to be put off. "I brought my own special blend on board again. The one you like."

It was bitter. Harsh in his belly. He hated it, and usually poured it out when she wasn't looking, but Ina was hard to refuse. Sometimes he wondered if she was in cahoots with the other women in his family who wanted to over-mother him. "I'd love a cup," he lied.

"Cream?"

Cream did it no earthly good, and it was a waste of good cream. "I'd love cream," he said, still forcing a polite smile.

That was all Ina needed to be pleased, as she rushed away to brew up her hideous potion, leaving Michael to take Sarah Collins's blood test. Well, that didn't matter, did it? It was a simple finger stick. Took ten seconds. But there was something about her…something that bothered him. Maybe it was the way she'd clung to him when in the elevator, or the little tingle he'd felt when they'd touched.

Or maybe it was the haunted look in her eyes. He knew that haunted look on a deeply personal level. Saw it in his own mirror sometimes.

Yes, that had to be it. Someone afraid. Someone numbed. He didn't often think about the battlefield these days, or all the wounded men he'd treated during those months on active duty. Grueling hours, hideous wounds. Another life altogether that he didn't allow to spill over into this one. What was done was done, and he wasn't going back. Now he worked on a cruise ship, drank insufferably bad tea with an overly protective surrogate mother and spent his off-duty hours in the lounge on the Lido deck, listening to bad karaoke and drinking diet cola.

"This won't hurt," he said to Sarah, as he pressed the barrel of the lancet device to the index finger on her left hand, then pushed the button to let the lancet prick her.

She flinched involuntarily, turning away her head when he squeezed a drop of blood from her finger and smeared it on the test strip. Probably squeamish, he decided. "Are you on this cruise with someone else?" he asked, as he counted down the seconds for the results to register. "Friend, family member, group tour?" *Spouse?*

"Alone," she said. "It's the best way to travel. You get to go where you want, do what you want. No compromises, no one impinging on your time."

Spoken like a true cynic, he thought. Or somebody badly burned by life. "One hundred and one," he pronounced. "I think you're good to go, so long as you don't overdo it."

Sitting up, then swinging her legs over the side of the bed, she said, "Believe me, I never overdo it."

"If anything, I suppose you could say that you underdo it. Which is why I'd like to have you check in here three times a day so I can do readings. For a couple of days anyway. And since there's always food available, I'd like to see you eating five or six times a day."

She laughed over that. "What you'd like to see and what I'm able to do are two entirely different things, Doctor. I'll take better care of myself until I get off the ship. That's a promise since I don't want to bother you again. But I'm afraid that doctor's orders are falling on deaf ears otherwise. I can't eat that many times a day."

"Small meals," he said. "Constant fuel for your body, so your blood sugar doesn't fluctuate so much." Was that a small spark of defiance flickering in her eyes now? Did the lady have a little challenge in her? "Unless you like being a patient in here. Because if you don't take better care of yourself, we're bound to meet under these very same circumstances again." Not that it would be a bad thing, the part where they met again, anyway. But he surely didn't want it to be under these circumstances. And now that he knew Sarah Collins was here, on the ship, all alone...

No! He didn't do that. Hadn't even been tempted before. He knew others of the crew indulged in little shipboard flings, but he didn't. Even though the emotional scars had long since healed from his last try at something more enduring than a casual fling, he didn't indulge at all now, and he was surprised that Sarah had brought out that little beast in him, especially with the resolution he'd made. Well, time to put the beast away. Michael Sloan was off the market, didn't look, didn't touch. Didn't anything! Not until he knew what came next for him.

"OK, so maybe you're right. But I don't like your prescription, Doctor, so here's my compromise. I'll eat my three meals a day, maybe have a small bedtime snack, but that's still up in the air, depending on how I feel at bedtime. And I'll stop in here once a day to have my gluco...blood-sugar level checked. Not the three times you wanted." She smiled sweetly at him. "That's my final offer."

"Most people don't defy doctor's orders." He liked it that she did.

"And most people don't go on a cruise to avoid social interaction, which is why I'm here, Doctor. To avoid social interactions, or even professional ones such as yourself. Once I get myself accustomed to the ship and its schedule, I'll be fine. I'm sure you'll be very busy tending patients who really want your attention once this cruise gets well underway, so there's no need to bother about me. I know how to take care of myself."

"No, you don't, or you wouldn't be lying here in my bed right now, arguing about it." He charted her latest blood-sugar result then set the clipboard on the stand next to the bed.

"I can't force treatment on you, and I'm not even going to argue with you about it. You know what I want, and it's up to you to decide how you want to take care of yourself. You can do it the right way, or…do whatever you want to do." With that, he spun around and walked away. No use arguing with her. She was already dead set on what she intended to do and, as pretty as she was, that didn't always translate into smart. Which seemed to be the case with Miss Sarah Collins.

Or maybe not. He couldn't tell. She'd be back, though. One way or another—following doctors orders, or going against them—she'd be back. He was counting on it.

Sarah returned to her cabin under the escort of a nurse named Ina. She was a nice sort, had even fixed her a decent cup of tea, which had hit the spot. Ina probably would have stayed to tuck her into bed, but Sarah opted for a shower in preparation for going for a late-night meal. OK, so she was going to be good and eat the way she was supposed to. Either that or have herself another time of it in the hospital, and while she certainly had nothing against the hospital—it looked to be magnificently equipped—she had a thing against medicine in general. Loved it, hated it, wanted it, wanted to avoid it.

Mixed feelings all the way around, and the best way to avoid that was to avoid the issue causing the problem. Which was why she'd eat, which was why she'd consent to one, *maybe* two blood tests a day. Her mother used to say something about an ounce of prevention being worth a pound of cure, and since with her condition a pound of cure came in the form of a hospital and a good-looking doctor, she would opt for the ounce of prevention. For a few days. Then she'd get off the ship and see what else she could find for herself. Maybe Japan. Or, better yet, Hong Kong. Nobody there would force food and blood tests on her.

After a quick shower, Sarah finally gave in and went off

in search of a light meal. Off the beaten path…not in any of the main dining rooms, or at the continual buffet of lobster and fruit and so many other delicacies it nearly caused her to go queasy thinking about all the choices. No, she stayed away from all the main sources and instead opted for a dark, cozy little lounge on the Lido deck where one of the passengers, who was a little too inebriated to show good sense, was attempting a tune on the karaoke, and doing a miserable job of it. He was singing about an anguished phantom and sounding more like a walrus with bellyache. Which suited Sarah's purposes as the lounge was practically empty.

She ordered a small salad and a cup of seafood chowder, and settled into one of the back booths to wait, trying hard not to listen to the off key warblings that were getting more off-key by the moment. Shutting her eyes, she leaned her head against the back of the booth, fighting away the image of the good doctor, which had been lingering there a while longer than was comfortable.

Bad impression, she decided. That's why she kept thinking about him. He'd made a bad impression on her. But the images there were anything but bad, which was why she decided to force her concentration on the second verse going on at the front of the lounge. More off key than the first. And much louder.

At the point where it became nearly unbearable Sarah decided not to wait around for her food. She wasn't hungry, and she could eat in the morning. So she opened her eyes, started to scoot out of the booth, only to be stopped at the edge of the seat by a large form she recognized from the sheer size of him, since in her little corner of the lounge it was too dark to see much of anything. "Spying on me?" she snapped.

He placed a cup of chowder down in front of her, along with her salad, then wedged himself into the seat right next to her, pushing her back from the edge. "Apparently, I am," he said, handing her a soup spoon.

CHAPTER TWO

"So, WHAT do you want, Doctor? What do you *really* want?" She was a little flattered by his attention, actually. It had been a long year avoiding everybody with whom she'd come into contact, and there were so many nights when she would have enjoyed a dinner companion, a male companion especially. No strings attached, separate checks, light conversation, going their separate ways at the end of the meal, of course. Someone to share a little space with her at the same table, someone staving off the appearance that she was so pathetically alone.

She wasn't antisocial, even though it appeared she was. Just cautious these days, as getting involved came easily to her. Easily, but with such a high price…costly mistakes she was bound to make again if the occasion arose. And she simply didn't trust herself to do otherwise, which was why she kept to herself now. "Did you follow me here, or do you moonlight as a waiter when you're off duty in the hospital? Are you serving up syringes of penicillin by day and dry martinis with a lemon twist by night?"

He laughed, raising his hand to signal the waitress. When he caught her attention, she gave him a familiar nod, then scurried off to the bar. "Some might think that's the same thing, one cure being as good as another. When you're on holiday, a ship has amazing opportunities, with so many things to do. But when you're on a ship for your employment as well as your living space, those opportunities are pretty limited and the space gets rather small, the longer you're confined to it. I don't fraternize with the guests in the planned social activities, don't date them, don't play shuffleboard with them, don't serve them drinks either. Most of the time I try to keep to places where there aren't so many people hanging around. Keep the separation between crew and guests intact. And right now this seems the place to do it."

"Sounds…dull. So many things to do, and here you are with me, probably the one and only avowed antisocial passenger on board. Not very interesting at all, Doctor. Not for a man who could have other choices, if he so wishes." She glanced at the waitress who was giving him an admiring appraisal, then at a table with three well liquored-up women, all of whom had that same look for him. It seemed the good doctor did have his opportunities if he cared to take them. "A number of other choices," she said.

"If you *want* those choices."

"And you don't?" She arched a curious eyebrow. "That surprises me."

"It surprises me too, sometimes. But it avoids a lot of complications in the long run and who needs complications when you can have all this?" He pointed to the karaoke singer standing under the dim blue light on the postage-stamp-sized stage, singing his off-key heart out.

"Sounds like a been there, done that to me. Once burned, twice shy, or something like that."

"It's that obvious?" He said that with a smile, but that wasn't at all the impression she was getting from him. There was something deep, something disturbing in his voice. Some sadness, maybe? Or wistfulness? It was a hauntingly familiar tone, and one she recognized from her own voice when she wasn't trying so hard to mask it with something lighter, something less truthful, the way Michael was trying to do.

Something compelled her to hear his voice again, to elicit that emotion from him once more, but as she opened her mouth to speak, the karaoke singer hit a particularly loud, startlingly sour note that caused even him to sputter, then giggle an apology into the microphone—but not quit singing.

Michael cringed visibly, and this time the smile that spread to his face was genuine. "You can see why there aren't so many people around here."

The moment was gone. It was too late to try and discover something she had no right to discover. "Well, I think earplugs are a good remedy," she said lightly, shaking off the building intensity and finally relaxing into the moment between them a little more. His motives seemed innocent enough, and she did understand how this was a good place to come if you were seeking solitude on a crowded ship— nice, dim room, secluded entryway making it easy to overlook, perfect low-key ambiance, comfortable booths arranged intimately so they gave the seeming appearance of aloneness. This one in particular, tucked in behind a column, was especially private, which was why she'd chosen it. For a moment it crossed her mind that this might be Dr Sloan's regular booth for all the same reasons she had taken to it. "Or maybe he could do with an adenoidectomy." Meaning the removal of the little piece of tissue located where the throat connected with the nasal passage. Often adenoids were the cause of nasal congestion, thick breathing or, in some cases, a nasal-sounding voice.

Michael shot her a curious look. "You know what an adenoidectomy is? I wouldn't think that's too common a term."

Her comment had been too medical, especially when she was trying to hide from everything that connected her to medicine in any way. But sometimes it just slipped out. Natural instincts coming back to haunt her. Well, that was a mistake she wouldn't repeat. "I don't suppose it is common but a friend of mine had it done," she lied. It had been a patient of hers, so in the longest stretch of the word maybe that hadn't been a lie after all. "Opened up her nasal passages quite nicely, helped her stop talking through her nose, breathing easier...." Too medical again. "You know. Whatever goes along with that kind of surgery." Sarah watched, out of the corner of her eye, to see if he believed her, which apparently he did because he turned his attention to the waitress who was on her way over to the table with a soda and a sandwich. She placed them on the table in front of him, bending much too close for anything other than what she had in mind, which had nothing to do with serving him food, practically slathering him with a come-hither smile. Of which he took no notice.

Most men, having it flaunted in their faces that way, would at least look, but Michael Sloan did not, which made Sarah wonder all the more about him.

Michael and the waitress chatted for a another moment about someone who worked in the business office—she still showing the same interest in him while he showed none in her—then when the waitress had decided that she was wasting her time she scampered away to wait on a another customer. That's when Michael returned his attention to Sarah. "It's like a little city here. Everybody knows everybody else's business."

Like the waitress who knew what Michael wanted even though he didn't have to order it? Briefly, Sarah wondered how much business the waitress and Michael knew about each other, and if his lack of a show of interest in her had been for appearances only. She was young, blonde, built the way every good plastic surgeon wanted his surgical enhancements to turn out. Of course, he'd already denied involvements or, as he called them, complications. Still, a man like Michael...good-looking, smart... She wondered. "The same way it is in a hospital," she said, trying to sound noncommittal.

"Do you work in a hospital?"

Damn. She'd slipped again, when she'd promised herself she'd be more careful. Twice inside two minutes. Something about him eased the tension right out of her, made her feel almost normal again, and she was going to have to be very careful around him. "No, but I like to watch those hospital shows on television. They're very…realistic. Make you feel like you're really there." Ah, the lie of it all, but the look of mild amusement on his face told her he'd bought her rather impaired explanation.

He chuckled. "Real life wrapped up in an hour, minus time out for commercials, once a week. Everybody gets cured or killed at the end, don't they? Or falls in love and lives happily ever after. Well, you are right about one thing. Gossip prevails in the hospital, too. Sometimes it can get so bad it's like it takes on an existence of its own."

"Which you can't live without?" she asked.

"That might be putting it too strongly. Personally, I can live without it quite nicely, like I can live without a good cup of strong, black coffee if one's not available to me. But for some people a little good gossip can start the day off with a bang, the way a good cup of coffee can."

"If you indulge," she said. Somehow, she didn't see him as the type.

"Which I don't. In the gossip, anyway. Can't say that I'd turn down a good cup of coffee, though."

She was glad he'd redeemed himself with that one because she didn't want to picture Michael Sloan as petty in any way, and gossip could be so petty. Being the brunt of it herself over her break-up with Cameron Enderlein, she knew. "So why did you choose a cruise ship?" she asked, knowing she probably shouldn't get that involved. But it seemed right to her. The mood between them was pleasant enough, his company nice. And she desperately missed companionship, not only in a personal way but in a medical one. It had been such a long time since she'd talked medicine with anybody, and while this wasn't going to go into any medical depth, it seemed harmless enough on a superficial level. An encounter with someone from her own profession was stimulating. Then, after tonight, she'd get lost in the ship's crowd, and he'd get busy in the ship's hospital, and that would be that. So it didn't matter. "Rather than a hospital or a clinic somewhere, why here?"

"It's a good job," he said, this time his voice the guarded one she'd already heard bits of before. "The facilities are excellent, patients are usually pretty nice, and I like the tropical islands. Oh, and the food is great." He picked up his sandwich and took a bite of something that looked to be a huge Cubano—pork, vegetables, and a whole lot of other ingredients that added up to one large meal between two pieces of bread.

And one large avoidance, too, she thought as she picked at her salad, finally spearing a grape tomato. But what was it to her? If he didn't want to tell her, she didn't care. They weren't friends, after all. They were barely acquaintances.

"So what kind of job do you do?" he asked, after he'd swallowed and taken a drink of his diet cola. "Wait…let me guess." He leaned back in his seat, folded his arms across his chest and studied her for a moment.

Studied her so hard she blushed under his scrutiny. Good thing the lights in here were dim and he couldn't see her reaction.

"I don't take you to be a lady of leisure," he said. "You've too much purpose in your eyes."

If only he knew how wrong he was. She'd been nothing but a lady of leisure for the past year, and there was absolutely no purpose in her eyes. Maybe once, but not any more.

"Am I right?" he asked, when she didn't respond to his first guess.

Rather than answering, she played his game and busied herself with her soup. If he could indulge himself in a little avoidance, so could she.

"So the lady isn't going to answer. Which means I'll have to take a wild guess. You're too short to be a fashion model, you don't eat with enough passion to be a chef, this is October, which is the middle of the school year so you're not a schoolteacher, and you're too pale to be a professional golfer."

"A golfer?" She laughed over that one. "Where did you come up with that?"

"I'm a doctor. I saw your muscles when I examined you. Very nice, but not overly developed. I can picture you swinging a golf club."

"I'll just bet you can," she said. "Sorry to disappoint you but I don't have a golf swing and I don't play golf. Never have."

"Well, that narrows the field down, doesn't it?"

"That ends the field, Doctor," she said, scooting toward the other side of the booth. This was entirely too enjoyable, and it would have been easy to spend another hour or two here, chatting about nothing and enjoying everything about it. Which was why she had to leave.

"Call me Michael, please," he said, not trying to stop her from leaving.

That surprised her a little. She'd expected a small protest from him, or maybe even an offer to walk her back to her cabin, which she might have taken him up on. But as she climbed out of her seat, he stood and offered a polite hand to her, then turned and signaled the waitress back over to refill his glass—both with the same insouciant effort. All casual, all impersonal, as was his goodnight to her.

"I want to see you in the morning for a finger stick," he said. "I'll be on duty at eight."

She nodded, offered him a half-smile, and scooted out of the lounge to a popular song being mutilated by a short, round, bald-headed Elvis impersonator who sounded like he needed an adenoidectomy, too.

* * *

She slept in, avoiding the morning finger stick, and when, at
nearly ten, she heard a knock on the cabin door, she assumed
it was Michael, coming to do her blood work. But she was
wrong. It was one of the ship's medical technicians. Cheery
smile, bright face, she was more than happy to poke Sarah's
finger. "It's a little low," Paulina Simpson said, showing the
monitor to Sarah, who read the blood-sugar result at sixty-
five. "You need to eat something," Paulina continued, fishing
some sort of breakfast bar out of her pocket. "Doctor Sloan
told me to bring this along, that you'd probably need it."

"Dr Sloan thinks of everything, doesn't he?" Sarah said
amiably.

"He's a good doctor. Most of the docs come and go, work
a few weeks here and there, but the cruise line likes Dr Sloan
because he keeps coming back. He's reliable. The patients
trust him and he does an outstanding job."

A bit of a crush from the med tech, too? Sarah wondered.

"And he's received commendations from the cruise line,"
the girl went on.

Well, so much praise on Michael's account was all well
and good, but that still didn't put Sarah in the mood to deal
with him. For what it was worth, she felt a little slighted,
being passed off to a tech when she'd expected the doctor to
come calling on her. "Well, tell Dr Sloan thank you for the
breakfast bar, but that I'm doing fine on my own and I no
longer require medical attention."

Paulina arched a puzzled eyebrow, then nodded. "He
said you'd say that, so he gave me this." She handed over
a slip of paper.

Sarah took a look at it, then handed it back. "Tell Dr Sloan
I don't need a diet guide, that I'm quite capable of eating what
I need, when I need it. But I appreciate his concern."

"He said you'd say that, too. So…" she pulled a small
glucose monitor from her other pocket and handed it to Sarah
"…he told me to give you this, so you can check yourself at

any time. Although he would like to take a daily reading of his own, just to see how you're doing."

Apparently, there was no getting away from Dr Michael Sloan, even when he wasn't present. If he went to all this fuss over a simple little case of hypoglycemia, she could only image how he'd react to a serious illness. Good doctor, she decided, adding her own silent praise to Paulina's as she remembered the days when she'd been at least that persistent with her own patients. "Tell Dr Sloan thank you for the glucometer, and that I'll use it. And that if he insists, I'll allow him to do an occasional test, too." She didn't really need it, but who was she to interfere with a doctor doing his duty?

Too bad he was hiding away on a ship, she thought as she unwrapped the breakfast bar. The world needed good doctors like Michael. Of course, she was hiding away on a ship too, wasn't she? And by most accounts she'd been a pretty good doctor herself.

It was turning into a long day, and the hospital was getting busy. Predictable conditions, the lot of them. Upset stomachs, seasickness, diabetic upheavals from people going wild over so much food available to them. People underestimated their stamina on a ship and he got to patch up the results. It was very different from general surgery, and sometimes he did long for the days when he'd spent his life in the operating theater.

But now… "Take two of these pills this afternoon, and two more before you go to bed. If you're still nauseated in the morning, come back and see me and we'll try something different." He handed the bottle to the fifty-something woman, and watched her leave the examining room, her face a little less green than it had been when she'd come in. "And no seafood for a couple of days," he called after her, remembering that this particular incident of gastric upset had come after a rather large consumption of lobster for lunch.

He couldn't blame her, really. Cruises were all about over-indulgence. Of course, there was Sarah, who wouldn't indulge at all. He was willing to bet she hadn't eaten a thing since her breakfast bar. She was a hard one to figure out. Last night, in the lounge, after she'd relaxed a little, she'd seemed like she had been enjoying his company. He'd certainly enjoyed hers. But just when things had finally slipped into a nice, casual mood, she'd upped and left him there. It wasn't his place to ask her questions, but he was curious. He saw all kinds of people on the ship. Lonely widows and widowers, people getting over the break-up of a relationship, people pressed with tough life decisions running away for a while to think. And people who were simply on holiday. As for Sarah, well, he wasn't sure where she fit in. Normally he was pretty good at telling, but he couldn't get a reading on her. Other than the fact that he liked her, and something about her drew him in, he simply didn't know.

One thing was certain, though. She didn't want a personal relationship in her life as much as he didn't want one in his. That alone made a shipboard friendship seem appealing. "Hello," he said to his next patient, as he stepped into the ex-amining room to have a look at a casualty of a volleyball game—a soft-looking fortyish man who didn't exercise at home but who took the opportunity to start once he'd hit the high seas. "I understand you hurt your back? Maybe twisted an ankle, too?"

The man, who was sitting on the edge of the exam table with his bare, skinny legs sticking out from under the sheet draped over his lap, nodded, looking up from his bent-over position. "Guess I'm a little out of shape." he admitted. "Haven't played in a while."

Michael wasn't going to ask how long that translated into. Instead, he took a look, diagnosed a few strained and sprained muscles and sent the man off to the spa to spend the after-noon in a whirlpool. It wasn't a precise medical therapy exactly, but why not give the man what he'd come for? Something he didn't have in his real life.

So, after what seemed like an interminably long day of routine aches and pains, Michael signed the next watch over to the following doctor on duty, a competent general practitioner named Reese Allen, and headed for his quarters. His leg ached a little more than usual, although it shouldn't, and it was time to get off it for a while. But as he walked down the corridor to his cabin, which was adjacent to the hospital, he changed his mind and caught the elevator up to the sundeck. He didn't actually get outside much on these cruises, and right now he felt the urge for a little sun on his face. And he knew the perfect place. It was amidships, in a little tuck-away behind one of the bars that didn't usually go into use until dark. There were a few deck chairs there, maybe three or four, and no one ever lounged there because there was no real view, unless you enjoyed looking at the back bar or the bottom side of the little rise holding the deck chairs with a perfect view of the pool. Good spot, he thought, heading off in that direction. Very good spot. He'd spend an hour, maybe two, go to the lounge and have Hector fix him a Cubano for supper, then…well, nothing came after that. He didn't make plans, although the thought of a little time spent with Sarah Collins suddenly popped into his mind.

It was a wish that came true almost immediately as he rounded the corner to his little tuck-away and found her in one of the deck chairs. Just her. Nobody else was around. She was there, stretched out almost elegantly in the chair, wearing a simple, one-piece black swimsuit that exposed beautiful long legs, even though they were pale. The black of the swimsuit complemented her black hair and the milky color of her skin was a startling, sexy contrast. Sarah had on black sunglasses, through which she was reading…he couldn't tell what, for sure. It looked like a copy of the *New England Journal of Medicine*, but she snapped it shut and tucked it into her big straw bag the instant she saw him. It was probably a fashion magazine, he decided as he headed toward her. Or another of the women's specialty magazines available from the ship's store.

She tilted her head down and gave him a long, cool glance up and over the top of her dark glasses before she finally spoke. "So, you *are* spying on me."

"I admitted it once, and I'm sticking to it."

"Have you come to do a blood test? You're so dedicated that you'll chase your patients down no matter where they're hiding?"

"I'd like to say yes but, unfortunately, I don't have my medical equipment with me. I'm afraid I'm off duty right now, too."

"Somehow, I doubt that you're ever *really* off duty," she said, that cool stare of hers continuing. It was cool, but not unfriendly. More like wary. "You strike me as one of those doctors who lives and breathes his work. Dedicated beyond reason. Otherwise why would you become a ship's doctor? I don't imagine you can ever really get away from it here, can you?"

"Actually, I have this little hiding place where I go so I *can* get away. No one knows about it, no one goes there, except…"

"Me?" she ventured. "Just like I know about your booth in the karaoke lounge?"

"It is funny, isn't it, how we keep bumping into each other in all the places no one else wants to go? You know, the secluded places."

"I'm antisocial," she reminded him with a hint of a smile tweaking her lips. "What's your excuse, other than you're spying on me?"

His leg was starting to ache even more now, that dull throb he despised that had never completely gone away, and he really needed to sit down. He hated it when this happened.

The reminder, the memories…of so many things he wanted to forget. *Damn, he hated it!* "My excuse is that I've been coming here for the better part of a year now."

She arched her eyebrows…beautifully sculpted eyebrows. Everything about Sarah Collins was beautifully sculpted, in fact. "Well, then, by all means, you should sit down."

"And interrupt you?"

"You're assuming that you being here would interrupt me."

"Would it?" he asked, summoning every bit of determination he had to fight off the inevitable limp that came when he was tired…fight it off long enough to take the last ten steps toward the deck chair next to her. Gritting his teeth, he took one step, then another. Sure, it was a vanity thing, being self-conscious like he was. There was no disgrace in his disability. But, damn, he had the right to hold onto a little vanity, didn't he? His limp caused questions, which required explanations. And the whole sordid story, once he'd explained it, brought pity, which he didn't want. Especially not from someone like Sarah Collins. So he took another few steps toward her, until he finally reached the chair. Then he sat, letting out an involuntary sigh of relief. Two hours off his feet, and he'd be fine. But one thing was sure—those two hours were going to be spent right here. He didn't have it in him to get up again. So if Sarah stayed, he'd spend them with her, and if she didn't stay…

"There's nothing to interrupt," she said. "I was doing exactly what you intend to do, enjoying a little sun well away from the crowds. Having someone else doing the same alongside me wouldn't be an interruption."

"But an intrusion, perhaps?" he asked, shifting to find a comfortable position.

"I don't think you're an intrusion. But if that becomes the case, I'll let you know." With that, she pushed her sunglasses up again, making her intention not to converse quite clear.

Then, out of the blue, "You don't snore, do you?" she asked. "Because if you do, that's an intrusion."

He chuckled. What was it about her that he liked so much? She put up walls, and she wasn't engagingly friendly either. Polite when interaction was forced on her but remaining at a distance. And so damned intriguing that he didn't even care if they spent the next two hours lounging next to each other without speaking a word.

The truth was, he liked Sarah Collins.

While she hadn't been looking for him, not consciously, on some unexplainable level she wasn't displeased that he'd found her. On a limited basis, Michael Sloan was rather pleasant company. Sarah found herself wishing, just a little, that she could talk in-depth about medicine with him, though. She'd just read a brilliant article in the *New England Journal* on advances in medication used to treat hypertension, and she would have loved some lively discussion on that with a colleague. But she had to remind herself almost daily that she'd left medicine behind her, then content herself with the void in her life that that decision had caused.

Unfortunately, the passion hadn't left her, which was why she wasn't engaging him this very moment. She stayed away from medicine because she could so easily be drawn back.

Although, as a doctor, she had noticed his limp. She hadn't stared, of course, especially with the way he had been trying so hard not to limp. Male ego, probably. In her experience as a doctor, the one thing she'd learned well was that men preferred to grit their teeth and bear it rather than admitting a weakness. Actually, that's what had almost killed Cameron. He'd been tired, he'd been losing weight. He'd blamed it on working too much, even though she'd asked him to have himself checked out. *And he a doctor!* Well, the dreadful truth had turned out to be leukemia. The other dreadful truth was that she should have insisted on him getting checked, then kept on insisting when he'd refused. Even tied him up and dragged him to a clinic, if she'd had to. But she hadn't. Probably because avoidance and denial had been easier.

Luckily for Cameron, his ending turned out to be a happy one in so many ways. He'd beaten his cancer, found a perfect wife and now they had a family.

It seemed, though, that the good doctor lying next to her right now was much the same as Cameron. Too stubborn, or too large an ego…she didn't know which. But it was on the tip of her tongue to say something to him. To ask him what was wrong, and if he'd sought medical attention. Which was none of her business. Still, he'd shown a sufficient amount of pain to someone with a trained eye, and whether or not she was calling herself a doctor these days, she was concerned. "Do you ever get time off?" she asked, not sure how to broach the subject without seeming too medical about it.

"Between cruises. A few days here and there."

"Nothing sustained, though? Maybe a few weeks where you can go and treat yourself to some real rest? On one of these tropical islands where we're going to stop on the cruise, perhaps?"

"Social worker," he said.

"What?"

"Last night, I was trying to figure out what you do. My guess right now is social worker. You show just the right amount of concern for other people's concerns, which would make you a very good social worker."

"Well, I'll take that as a compliment because I admire anyone who has the dedication to be a social worker but, no, that's not what I do. And I'm not a librarian either, if that was going to be your next guess."

"I might have. I've always thought librarians have a smoldering, secret sensuality about them, which fits you."

Sarah laughed. "Nothing smoldering in me."

"But there is, Sarah. It's there, and you do a nice job of hiding it, which is why you'd make a good librarian. They have that reserved exterior, but on the inside—"

"Let me guess," she interrupted. "When you were young you had a secret crush on a librarian."

"Not so secret. Her name was Mrs Rowe, and the way she pinned up her red hair, and those tight tweed skirts she wore…" Michael faked a big shiver. "I used to check out books every day. Big books, adult books that I thought made me look intelligent and old. As many as I could get in my canvas bag, like I thought she believed I was taking them home and reading them every night. I was eight, by the way."

"So what brought an end to the love affair?"

"After a couple of weeks, Mrs Rowe asked me if I wouldn't rather have books from the children's section, then she handed me one about a precocious monkey and told me I'd do better with that than the one on quantum physics I was attempting to check out."

"She was probably right, unless you were a child genius."

"Not even close."

"Then I'd say Mrs Rowe had good insight."

"And a good figure, too," he commented under his breath.

Sarah laughed. "Not to be missed, even by a boy of eight." Which further proved her theory about men. They were not all alike, as some people said, but they were certainly similar in some ways. Even now, as he shifted in his deck chair, she saw a little grimace of pain on his face, yet, come hell or high water, he wasn't about to admit it.

Well, back to the original premise and she was sticking to it. It was none of her business.

She was still concerned, though.

CHAPTER THREE

SARAH hadn't planned on going ashore, yet when the passengers started to leave the boat to spend a few hours browsing the shops, seeing the sights and eating the food in Nassau, on New Providence island in the Bahamas, she'd changed her mind and followed along after them. Her cabin was small and she wasn't enjoying her private time there as much as she'd thought she would. While it wasn't her intention to join in with any of the activities on board ship, she wasn't exactly avoiding some minor mingling…walking about, nodding a pleasant hello here and there, making idle chat where it was necessary.

Something about the sea air had caused this change in her, she supposed as she took one last look in the mirror before she dashed out the door, amazed that in only two days she'd taken on a little color. She'd probably gained a pound or two, too, since eating seemed to be the number-one cruise pastime for just about everybody, and the good doctor did keep watch over her to make sure she did her fair share. Michael deserved his due credit, though. Her blood sugar had been perfect three checks in a row now, and she was actually feeling better—not so tired all the time. His vigilance reminded her to take care of herself. That was the reason she was going off the ship this afternoon. For the first time since she couldn't remember when she actually wanted to take a walk, soak up some of the local culture. Her past holidays had been lackluster affairs overall, where she'd showed mild interest at best and, more commonly, no enthusiasm whatsoever, and while she wouldn't go so far as to admit to any enthusiasm over this little outing, she wasn't dreading it as much as she could have.

Too bad Michael wouldn't be coming along. At least, she didn't think he would be. What he'd told her at the start of the cruise, that he didn't usually fraternize with the guests, was holding true. She'd seen him only in passing since they'd spent a couple of quiet hours together in the deck chairs, and even her blood tests were done by somebody else and reported to Michael who, in turn, relayed messages back to her through somebody else.

Well, it didn't matter, really. She would have enjoyed spending more time with him, catching the edge of a medical conversation where she could, but it didn't seem that it was meant to be. Admitting she was disappointed was an exaggeration, but in all honesty she wouldn't have objected to bumping into him on the docks. As it turned out, however, a casual enquiry of the medical technician who'd last tested her blood revealed what Sarah wanted to know—the medical crew probably wasn't leaving ship at this port of call.

Oh, well…

Once Sarah was off the ship, she had several choices. She could see the area by taxi, take a walking tour, hire a horse-drawn carriage, or the one that appealed to her the most—take a jitney, a small bus overcrowded with locals. It made frequent stops, went to the areas the tourists avoided, and she was in the mood for that. She didn't want to shop, didn't want to see the museums or the city's renowned colonial architecture. She didn't even want to go have a dolphin encounter—swimming or snorkeling with trained dolphins—which was a very popular attraction. Instead, she wanted to ride, and watch. Meaning, be alone again. But that was fine. It was a beautiful day, the air was warm, and this sure beat staying in her cabin, reading another medical journal.

So Sarah caught the jitney, and was rather amazed by it. Bright green, small, and chugging along loudly and smokily, like it was about to roll over and die at the side of the road, it wasn't comfortable transportation, but the thirty or so people squeezed into a space that should have accommodated twenty or so didn't mind the inconvenience. In fact, they all got rather chummy as the bus bumped its way through town, stopping at various street corners, letting people out, then letting other people back on.

From her rear seat which she shared with a plump woman named Mimmie and her chubby son who answered to the name Delroy, Sarah stared through the bus window at tourists scurrying into the various shops, some on the tourist map, some not. They were lining up at the doors of all the recommended cafés, happy to queue simply to have a taste of the local food, and flock into the Straw Market for the best of the best souvenirs. After fifteen minutes of being pinched against the side of the jitney, though, with Delroy smearing his sticky red lollipop up and down her arm, Sarah decided it was time to get off and find something better to do. Maybe take a walk through the botanical gardens.

So, at the next stop, she managed to squeeze her way past Mimmie and force herself through the standing passengers until she was down the aisle and out the door. Mimmie followed right behind her, though, with Delroy, who made sure his lollipop came into contact with the back of Sarah's white shorts at least five times. But once they were on the sidewalk, and Sarah was sure Delroy's candy was not attached to her shorts, she started to head down a side street, paying more attention to a street map than she was to her surroundings. Behind her, when she heard the sound of the jitney rev its clanking engine, she assumed it to be off on its route, but all of a sudden the sound of a horn, followed by screams of hysterical men and women, split the air.

Her maps slipped from her fingers and slid to the ground as Sarah spun around.

What was going on? It was hard to tell from where she was, but multitudes of people were running to surround the jitney, and those on the bus were scurrying to get off. And Mimmie…Sarah caught a glimpse of the woman trying to shove her way through the crowd, screaming at them, crying, pounding people aside with her fists.

Warning hairs on the back of Sarah's neck prickled and she immediately broke into a run, pushing herself past even more people crowding in to see whatever was happening. When she reached the jitney, she was still at the rear of the congested knot, but even from there she heard someone shouting about the little boy. Then a blood-curdling scream pierced the noise of the crowd. "Delroy!"

"Let me through!" Sarah cried. "I'm a doctor."

Some people moved for her, others didn't. "Let me through," she cried again. "I have to get through. I'm a doctor!"

All of a sudden, the crowd stepped aside for her, almost creating a corridor that led her straight to the front of the bus where Delroy laid sprawled, unconscious, most of the way under the bus, with only his toes sticking out. His mother was on her knees at his side, wailing, pulling on him, trying to get him free.

"Don't," Sarah warned her. But Mimmie was so frightened she was comprehending nothing but her son's dire injury. "Don't move him," Sarah said anyway. Once she'd dropped to her knees she immediately checked Delroy for a pulse. A quick press to the femoral artery in his groin, which was the only pulse point she could reach without actually crawling under the bus, did reveal a pulse, but not a good one. It was thready, cutting in and out like his heart was deciding whether it wanted to keep beating or quit. "He's alive," she told Mimmie, who was still tugging on Delroy's arm.

She had to get the woman to stop. "Somebody, please, don't let his mother move him," she called to the crowd. "I need help here. I need someone to hold his mother back." With that, two women jumped forward and wrapped arms around Mimmie, forcibly pulling her away from her son. She struggled for a moment then, with big tears rolling down her cheeks, looked pleadingly at Sarah. "Please, *please*, help him!"

"He's alive," she told the woman. "But he can't be moved."

"He must come out from under the bus."

"No, he has to stay where he is." There was no time to explain, no time to waste trying to calm a tortured mother when the pulse she was feeling under her fingertips was fluttering even more tentatively now. "I need an ambulance," she cried to the crowd, not sure what the procedure was in Nassau. Then she bent down, pressed her cheek to the black pavement to see what she could of the little boy.

Nothing was trapped under the bus tire. That was good. But he was pressed very close to it, just inches away, with his shirt actually caught under the tire, and nothing about him was moving. That was bad. Head injury, perhaps? At the very least, internal damage. And here she was without a medical kit. This was the first time she'd regretted that since she'd left her practice. Funny thing was, it was still intact, still packed with all the necessities, sitting just inside her apartment ready to go, like it had always known she'd back for it someday.

Today was that day! And now she had to get closer, had to have a look before anybody touched the child or moved him. So, without another thought, Sarah got down on her belly and inched her way slowly along the pavement under the bus, trying all the while to forget that she'd been claustrophobic lately. Her hands were shaking, her head going light…all the classic signs of a panic attack coming on. Except she couldn't do that. Had to get control. Had to save a life.

Breathe, Sarah.

She inched even farther in, stopping every second or two, taking a look at what she could see from her angle, feeling for a pulse point, running her fingers lightly over the boy's body for an assessment.

You're the doctor. This child needs you. She couldn't let him down. Wouldn't.

As she moved her way alongside his limp body, she saw that Delroy still clutched the red lollipop in his hand, and that caused a hard lump to form in her throat. "We're going to get you out of here, Delroy," she said to the boy, even though he wasn't conscious. "Then take you to a hospital, where they'll give you a brand-new lollipop. Is red your favorite color? I like green." She felt stickiness over his abdomen, and was sure it wasn't from his lollipop. Hopefully, it was only blood from a cut, and nothing significant.

His breathing was shallow and rapid, and her own breaths were fighting against her, trying to go shallow and rapid, too. *Don't quit now, Sarah. You can do this.* "When my mother used to buy a bag of lollipops, my sister and I always fought over who got the red ones, even though I really wanted the green ones. But because Annie wanted the red, so did I. Do you have any brothers or sisters, Delroy?"

She was nearly at his shoulder now, sickened by the twist of his right arm. It was a bad break, easy to diagnose even from her awkward position. Not a compound fracture, though, thank God. No broken skin, no bone sticking out. But it would require surgery. She couldn't even imagine how many bones had been crushed in his little arm, and there was no way to tell. "Looks like you're going to have to use your left hand for your lollipops for a while," she said, doing a second check of his arm just to make sure she hadn't missed an area where the bone might have been protruding. Under here, in the dark, it was hard to tell, but her second check confirmed her first impression.

Pulling herself a little closer to Delroy, Sarah reached across his body, trying as best as she could to make an assessment of other injuries, but it was difficult, given that she was so far away and still in such an awkward position. She decided that once she reached his head she'd try to get over to the other side to do the same exam as she'd done on the right side.

"Pupils?" someone called from behind her. Somewhere not under the bus.

"Haven't assessed them yet. Don't have a light." The voice was familiar, but it was hard to tell through the noise of the crowd.

"It's on its way," the man shouted. At that moment a small flashlight was thrust, with some force, under the bus, and she grabbed it, grateful that a medic had finally arrived on the scene. Now, if only she had enough room to push herself up to her knees for this. But she didn't. This was an exam she had to do either on her belly or her side.

"Are you medical?" he yelled. "Do you need help under there?"

Was it Michael? It sounded like him, and she prayed that it was. She needed someone she trusted, needed someone who was calm to help her get through this. "Michael Sloan?" she called. "It's Sarah. Sarah Collins, from the ship." Gently pushing back one of Delroy's eyelids, she flashed the light in his eye to see pupillary reaction. She studied it for a moment, then did the same for his other eye. Not responsive to light. A very bad sign. "I think we have a head injury here. His pupils aren't equal and reactive to light. He also has a broken arm, not a compound fracture, though. At least, that's the best I can tell. And that's all I can see so far. Oh, and there's not enough room for two of us."

"Sarah," he called, crouching at the edge of the bus.

She glanced at him for a moment, glad to see his face, even though it was streaked with worry. "I don't suppose I mentioned that I'm a doctor, did I?" she asked, knowing full well she hadn't. These days, if it didn't come up in conversation, she didn't bring it up. Even in the company of another doctor. *Especially* in the company of another doctor. That made avoidance all the more easy.

"Do you need a cervical collar?" he called back, rather than responding to her confession.

"To get him out, yes. And a backboard." She did a quick check of Delroy's pulse. Weaker. In her gut she knew he had internal injuries, too, some kind of bleeding somewhere, but she couldn't get a good feel of his belly to check for rigidity. "And I think he's bleeding inside, so I'll need an IV set-up ready to go once he's out of here."

"But he's breathing?"

"Shallow, rapid. Do you have a blood-pressure cuff?" she called, on the off chance that Delroy's other arm wasn't broken and she could take a blood-pressure reading.

Within seconds, a blood-pressure cuff and stethoscope were tossed under to her. But she was on the wrong side to use them, so she scooted all the way around the boy's head and over to the left of his body, praying that his injuries there weren't so extensive. A quick check of his arm revealed it she was safe to use the cuff, so she fastened it on, pumped it up then took a reading. "Damn,' she muttered, not hearing a thing. She tried it again. "Eighty over forty," she finally called. Deathly low. She desperately needed to get an IV into Delroy, to give him fluid volume to offset the internal bleed she guessed was causing his blood pressure to bottom out. "What are my chances for an IV right now, before we move him?"

"None," Michael called. "We've got assistance en route, but it's going to take a while."

"MAST?" Even as she asked, she knew that anti-shock trousers would not be available. Once they went onto the patient and were inflated, they tamped off the internal bleed and kept the blood pressure a little more stable.

"No."

"Other options?"

"Is he ready to move?"

"Not until he's stabilized. So far I've got a head injury, a critical break to his right arm and I have a feeling it might be compartmentalized." Bleeding inside the bone. "And I'm thinking there could be internal damage. And I haven't checked all of him." The boy's last minutes were ticking away, she feared. Moving him would almost surely kill him if she didn't get him stabilized, yet there was no way to stabilize him under the bus. "Look, Delroy," she said, wiggling herself close to his ear. "What I need for you to do is fight this. Really fight it. It's going to take us a while to move you, but we're going to get you to the hospital as soon as we can. So don't give up. You fight this, and I promise I won't leave you."

"We need to get him out from under there and have him ready for when the medics arrive," Michael called.

"Can we get the driver to move the bus?" Delroy's best chance was to be completely away from the bus so when ambulance arrived they could get right to the emergency care, but she wasn't willing to risk his life by pulling him out. As fragile as his pulse was now, and as shallow as his breathing had become, that would mean sure death. She didn't know that for sure, of course, but that was her gut feeling and for now she was going to go with her gut feeling.

"It's too dangerous. One wrong turn…. Are you're sure there's no room for me under there?" Michael called back. "Maybe with two of us bracing him…"

"No room." She wished there was room, but that simply wasn't the case. She trusted Michael out there, though. Even though he seemed so far away, she trusted his presence, trusted his judgement, trusted his opinions. He made her feel…safe, like everything was going to be fine. When that feeling finally took hold, all the panic inside her that had been bubbling up to the surface getting ready to explode simply vanished. She needed that. Needed it desperately. "Look, Michael, I know you said it's too dangerous, but you've got to find someone to drive the bus off us."

"No way in hell," he called. "That's crazy!"

"We'll be fine." Funny how she sounded like the calm one now. "There's enough clearance room." Barely, but it could work.

"The driver's sitting on the sidewalk, sobbing. He can't drive. I *don't want* him to drive."

"Then find somebody else who can. We can't bring Delroy out in his condition, but we need better access to him. So find somebody to get the bus off us."

"Sarah, no! That could get both of you killed if something goes wrong."

"What kind of doctor were you before you were on the ship?" Honestly, she didn't know, and it was an odd time to ask, but she had a hunch about him.

"Surgeon," he yelled back.

Just as she'd thought. Nerves of steel. He was the one to do it. "You do it, Michael. *You* get the bus off of us. Because if you don't…well, you know the consequences." She waited for him to refuse, but there was no response for a minute. So she worked her way down the left side of Delroy's body, finding what she thought was a broken femur. It just kept getting worse and worse for the poor child. "Well?" she finally called out to him.

"Look, Sarah, I don't want to do this. But I've got to trust that you know what you're doing."

Like she trusted that he knew what he was doing.

"I was getting the keys. So now tell me what you see on the bus. Your proximity to the wheel. Clearance above you."

Sarah gingerly rolled over on her back and looked up at the undercarriage. She wasn't a mechanic, didn't know what was what, but she was a good judge of distance, and this distance was much less than she'd guessed. "Eighteen inches clearance in most places. And as we lie here, the child has about twelve inches to his left, which would be the driver's side. He's not touching the tire, but it's close, and I can't get him lined up and any further away from it. Also the tires are turned to the left and the one on the driver's side tire is sitting in bit of a pothole, so before you move you'll have to straighten the tires or you'll run over his leg. And his leg is already fractured, I just discovered." Sarah drew in a steadying breath, counting, more now than ever, on Michael's calm composure to get her through this. "There's more clearance on the right side. You'll be fine there." But it was so close on the left, she wondered if an inexperienced jitney driver could do it.

"And where will you be during this?"

"I'll get back in line with his head." That was the best place, as coming back alongside of him would only increase the risk of her getting run over. "Have you ever driven a bus, Michael?"

"No."

"A car?"

"Yes?"

"A big car?"

"Does a big truck count?"

Sarah scooted on her left side, making her way back up along Delroy's body, aiming for a position where they would be head to head. As she scraped her way along the rough pavement, it was only then that she realized if Michael turned even a fraction of an inch in the wrong direction, he could run over them both and there would be no one to stop him. By the time she could yell directions to someone on the outside who would yell directions to him, it could be too late. But there wasn't another choice. Right at this moment she had to trust Michael like she'd never trusted another person in her life. And after so long of not trusting anything or anyone, it felt good. Surprisingly good.

"Look, Sarah, why don't you come out from under there and let me see what I can do. Maybe someone else out here can drive the damned bus…"

"I promised Delroy I wouldn't leave him, and I'm not going to?" This point was not negotiable. Amazingly, Michael didn't argue about it, like she'd expected he might. She liked it that he listened to reason. In her estimation that made him a much better doctor than she already knew him to be because he knew the value of giving support to your patient no matter what the situation.

Now all she needed was for him to be a good driver, too.

Suddenly a flashlight scanned the area from behind her. She couldn't turn to look at it even though she desperately wanted to see his face again. But she couldn't get herself into that position while he assessed his so-called surgical field before he performed this most critical operation. "So, what's your assessment, Dr Sloan?" she asked, trying to sound light about it. "Minor surgery required? Or major surgery?" After this was over, she'd need a *real* holiday.

"Major surgery, I'm afraid. Your *bit* of a pothole is a little larger than I thought, and it's going to be a problem."

"Meaning?"

"Meaning I've got to gun the engine to bump out of it. The driver's called his company to send a qualified driver out to do this, so maybe we should wait."

"But how long will it take for him to get here? I don't think we have time to wait." She listened for a moment and heard the far-off wail of a siren. The ambulance? She desperately hoped so.

"A few minutes," he said. "Look, Sarah, this is too dangerous…"

"I know the risks, Michael. We're running out of time, though, and I trust you to do this." She placed her fingers to the pulse in Delroy's neck. "So please trust me when I tell you that we have to get this done now. We're losing ground under here."

Michael didn't respond for a second, but finally he exhaled in an audible sigh. "Then I guess we don't have a choice, do we?" he said, snapping off his flashlight.

"No, we don't." Steadying herself for what was to come, Sarah put a reassuring hand on Delroy. "It's almost over," she said to the boy. "Just another minute, and they'll have this bus off us then we'll get you to the hospital." She said a silent prayer that it would be soon because as she laid her hands on Delroy's head, her fingers went to the pulse in his neck yet again. It was even weaker. Irregular now. In another few minutes there would be no pulse.

"Brace yourself," Michael called. "I'm not familiar with the gears, so this could be a little rough. But you'll be fine."

She raised her head just enough to see his feet as he walked away. *Well, Sarah, for someone who said she'd never work again as a doctor, you've sure jumped back into it in a big way.*

Shutting her eyes, she laid her face to the pavement and stretched both her arms ahead of her to make contact with Delroy as the bus's gears engaged. Then she drew in a deep breath and held it.

"Damn," Michael muttered, climbing into the jitney driver's seat. Of all the people in the world, it had to be Sarah under there! And why the hell hadn't she bothered telling him she was a doctor before now?

It was odd, but he didn't have time to think about any of it because there was a critically injured kid down there. And Sarah. And here he was at the wheel of a vehicle he'd never been inside before, let alone driven, scared to death, and ready to drive it anyway, no thanks to the real driver, who was still incoherent, getting more and more hysterical by the minute. Naturally, no one in the crowd had admitted to knowing how to drive one of these things either, of all the rotten luck. So there he was. In the hot seat, quite literally.

Damn! All he'd wanted to do was come ashore for a conch fritter from Clarice's Café and do a quick check of her daughter's leg.

Those things didn't take nerves of steel. This did, and as he studied the gears, trying to figure which did what, he forced himself not to think about the fact Sarah was a doctor who, for some strange reason, hadn't disclosed that fact to him. *Gears. Concentrate on the damned gears!*

That's exactly what Michael did for the thirty seconds before he jumped off the bus and dropped to his knees to tell Sarah what he'd decided. "I'm going to move the bus forward, rather than going backwards—it'll give me better momentum to pop the wheels out of the pothole. I just wanted you to know that the entire jitney's going to roll over you so you'll be prepared. Oh, and after it does, I'll expect an explanation."

"An explanation?"

"Of why you didn't tell me you are a doctor."

Michael didn't wait for her response to that. Instead, he climbed back into the jitney, sucked in a deep breath, turned the steering-wheel until the tires were straight, then depressed the clutch slowly, giving the engine enough gas to rock it, but not enough to get the tire out of the rut. He was too cautious. He knew that. But he lived cautiously these days. Still, he had to try it again, skip the caution and get it right. Sucking in yet another deep breath, Michael gave it another go, punching the gas pedal much harder this time. The bus rocked forward even harder, but still not enough. Damn it, it wasn't going to work! To get up the momentum he needed, he'd have to practically floor the gas pedal, and in doing so, the tire would pop out. But in that moment the bus would also be totally out of his control. And Sarah... He forced that thought from his mind, replacing it with another.

"I need help," he shouted, jumping from the jitney. "I need people to push this bus forward. Enough people to get behind and push it when I hit the gas pedal." This would work. He knew it! "Push it just enough so that we can get the front tire out of the hole."

Immediately, the majority of the hundred or so people who'd gathered there to watch ran to the back of the bus. Too many, of course, but he'd get a good line of men from the group, and that would do nicely. With the sound of the siren getting closer, he guessed they'd just about make it by the time the medics arrived.

"Damn," he muttered, steeling himself for what he had to do. Battlefield surgery had been easy compared to this.

The first time the jitney engine revved, Sarah held her breath, but nothing happened. The second time, she actually looked up, saw the bus try to move forward, then sit itself back down in the hole. Delroy was struggling for breath now, and it occurred to her that if he quit breathing altogether, she was in no position to attempt any sort of resuscitation. She'd have to pull him out from under the jitney, risking injuries that might kill him to perform CPR. "Just another minute," she said to the boy. "In fact, maybe we should count it off together."

She glanced out to the feet of the crowd. They were running away now. She couldn't imagine why. Clearing a way for the ambulance? It still didn't sound so close, but she hoped the people out there were making way for it. "One. Two. Three." She counted long, drawn-out seconds, thinking about Michael in between the protracted count, conjuring up his image, trying to find his sense of calmness. She didn't want to get to sixty and depended on Michael's distraction to keep her away from it because she feared that at sixty Delroy would give up for good.

Back in the driver's seat, Michael depressed the gas pedal and the crowd at the rear started to push. It took only a second for the wheel to come out of the hole, then he inched the bus forward, deathly afraid that he lacked the proper sensitivity in his right foot to do this. Actually, his right prosthetic foot. He could drive just fine, but the reflexes governing the movement in a prosthetic leg certainly weren't like those of a real leg, and he'd had more than his fair share of speeding tickets where he'd depressed the gas pedal too hard, trying to figure out the delicate adjustments to life without a limb. So, as sweat beaded across his forehead, he drove, hoping he was better than he gave himself credit for.

The jitney moved forward slowly and, thank God, went as straight as an arrow. At least his steering wasn't impaired, he thought as he looked into the rear-view mirror to see if he'd cleared Sarah and Delroy yet. He'd instructed the crowd not to converge on them, and so far everybody was hanging back. But he didn't see them yet, even though it seemed like he'd driven miles.

His hands ached from the way he gripped the steering-wheel—white knuckles all the way. And the sweat dripping down his face stung his eyes. If muscles could scream, the ones knotting in his shoulders and neck would do that as he forced the bus forward, willing himself to concentrate on the driving and not on Delroy. Not on Sarah.

"Eyes forward," he warned himself, even though he wanted to look in the rear-view mirror again, wanted to finally see them lying on the ground, safe and secure. "Eyes forward. Keep it steady." Just another few feet. That's all it was. All it could be. Just another few feet…another few inches.

Michael drove until he heard cheers coming from the crowd, yet even then he didn't look in the mirror until he'd driven well past the place where Sarah and Delroy were stretched out. When he finally came to a stop and applied the brakes, he slumped over the steering-wheel for a few moments, willing himself to breathe normally again, willing his heart to settle back down. Then and only then did he gamble a look at the two forms lying on the ground. And when he'd finally convinced himself that he hadn't run over them, it took him another few seconds to force himself out of the driver's seat.

Once he was out the jitney door, Michael was greeted by the cheers of the crowd...*they were actually cheering him*. But he ignored them in his haste to make his way back to Sarah. When he reached her, he dropped to his knees and began an immediate assessment of Delroy.

A glance out of the corner of his eye caused him to turn his head to Sarah. "You OK?" he asked, trying to sound unaffected by the whole event, even though the sight of her there on the ground affected him in ways he hadn't expected. She'd been so...vulnerable. And so trusting. Her mistake. People shouldn't trust him. He'd proved that a long time ago and so far nothing in his life had changed. He wasn't worthy of being trusted. Just ask the loved ones of the two men who'd trusted him to save their lives, and he hadn't. Those were families who knew just how far that trust went, where he was concerned.

"I'm fine," she said, pushing herself to her knees. "But I was wondering, were you following me again? Or do we just have this uncanny ability that makes us turn up at the same place at the same time?"

Uncanny, maybe. Something he was going to have to avoid in the future, definitely.

"Is the hospital good?" Sarah wrung her hands, watching the ambulance pull away with the patient she'd held onto for the past thirty minutes...thirty minutes that had seemed like a lifetime.

"Actually, yes. Prince Hospital has about four hundred beds, I think. It's the public hospital here, and they have just about every service you can imagine—general practice, surgery, obstetrical, emergency, intensive care. Delroy will be in good hands there, and if they feel they don't have all the support he needs, they'll transfer him to one of the hospitals in the States."

"If he lives," she said despondently.

"He'll live." Michael brushed away a dead twig that had tangled in her hair. "So, why didn't you tell me you were a doctor? Here I was, explaining hypoglycemia and all its complications to you, and you're a… What kind of medicine do you practice?"

"I don't practice medicine now, but when I did I specialized in internal medicine and family practice as a partner in an immediate care clinic."

"But you quit?"

He seemed to want an explanation, but she didn't talk about it. Not to anyone. "Burned out," she said. It was a simple explanation and people accepted that much better than they would the real reason. "Probably wasn't meant to be a doctor in the first place so I got out of it."

"Well, you sure could have fooled me, because the doctor under the bus seemed like someone who *should* be a doctor. Someone who cared enough to risk her life."

"Well, we all have our opinions, don't we?" That seemed a little snappish maybe, but she didn't want to talk about it. Not with Michael, not with anyone else. Right now she just wanted to go back to the ship, clean herself up, grab something to eat, and spend the rest of the day in her cabin. "Look, I'm sorry. I don't mean to be rude, but after what just happened…"

"I totally understand about the way you feel. Not about why you left medicine. But if you don't want to tell me, I won't ask. OK?" He frowned. "Are you aware that you're in need of some medical attention? I mean, a doctor would be, but as you're not a doctor now…"

"Really subtle, Michael. But I'm still not going to talk about it." She glanced down to the cuts and scrapes all over her legs and arms. "And I'm fine. When I get back I'll stop by the ship's hospital for some antibiotic ointment and bandages."

"Well, as you're not a doctor and I am, I'd like to get all the dirt washed off those cuts before that," he said, pointing to the hose-drawn carriage making its way down the opposite side of the street. "The streets aren't very clean here, in case you didn't notice."

He was attempting to humor her, to lighten her mood. Trying hard. Charming. Close to being irresistible. But she had to resist. That's what she did now…resisted. "I don't see any kind of facility nearby, so I'll be fine until I get back."

"Right there," he said, pointing to a picturesque little café not three doors away. "I was on my way to make a house call there anyway, so if you don't mind going with me…"

She glanced at the horse clip-clopping its way by her, then at the scrapes on her knees. She really didn't want to go, but there was no telling what was already festering in her wounds. And, yes, that was the doctor in her prevailing on her common sense. Wasn't it amazing, though, how Dr Michael Sloan always seemed to be on the spot when she needed him? Funny, how that worked out.

Funny, but nice. "OK, I'll go with you. But no doctor questions."

Taking her arm, he pulled her through the crowd of people that was finally beginning to disperse. Admittedly, she liked the feel of clinging to him. He was sturdy, and she hadn't had that in a very long time. It felt good.

"Are you being mysterious or stubborn?" he asked, as they approached the cottage door.

"I said no questions."

"You said no *doctor* questions. That wasn't a doctor question."

She glanced up at the smile spreading across his face. Yes, this felt good. Maybe too good.

CHAPTER FOUR

"YOU'RE the one who rescued Mimmie's boy, aren't you?" Clarice Rolle's high-pitched voice drifted over the noisy crowd while she ushered Sarah and Michael through the tiny café at the front of the wood-frame building. It was filled to capacity with people staring at Sarah, many of them patting her on the back and smiling as the three of them made their way down a hall and through a door into Clarice's living quarters in the rear. It was all very cozy—the café, the flat. Tidy, and immaculately clean, it was a nice, friendly place that Sarah immediately liked, both parts to it done up in different shades of blue—the café in an array of bright blues and the flat in more subdued shades.

"I was under the bus with him," Sarah admitted to Clarice, wishing she wasn't the center of attention now. Although an admission wasn't necessary with the way she looked. She was a mess, head to toe, covered in a mixture of dirt and blood and whatever else had come off the street, all of it ground into her tattered clothes, into her hair, her skin.

"Well, it was a brave thing going to help him like you did, when you could have been hurt yourself," Clarice said, giving Michael a frown and a shooing gesture that told him he clearly was not wanted or welcomed in the bedroom into which Clarice was leading Sarah. Once she'd shut the door, practically in his face, she said, "Now, you go clean yourself up in the bathroom, take care of those cuts and scrapes all over you, and I'll go and find you some fresh clothes to put on."

"That's not necessary," Sarah said, for the first time noticing that the leg of her shorts was split right up the middle, almost to her hip line. It was, quite literally, hanging in shreds, revealing much more of her leg than she cared to reveal. "I can just wash off."

"With your clothes hanging on you the way they are, showing off more than they cover now, I don't think you'll want to walk through the streets that way. Men being what they are, and this is such a crowded town with all the ships docking here…" She gave her head a wary shake and pointed to Sarah's knit shirt, which was torn halfway down from her neckline. "But don't you worry. We're about the same size, so I've got something you can put on." Clarice said, "and it wouldn't be polite of me not to take care of you after what you did for Mimmie's boy."

Sarah studied Clarice for a moment. It was optimistic, thinking they were about the same size. Clarice had a perfect figure, and she was diminutive, the way Sarah had always wanted to be. Sarah, in comparison was…larger. Taller, bigger bones, bigger everything. But Clarice was right about the way she looked. Her clothes were so close to being indecent, with so many rips, and covered by so much blood. "Thank you," she finally said. "I'd appreciate it. And I'll be glad to pay you—"

"That's not the way we do things here," Caprice interrupted. "We take good care of our friends, and you're a friend now."

"A friend," Sarah murmured, shutting the bathroom door. It had been a while since she'd considered anybody a friend, or even been anybody's friend. Cameron had been the last, and look what she'd done to him. Even thinking about that ugly period in her life caused her hands to shake as she turned on the water in the sink, then splashed some of it in her face. She couldn't think of it…wouldn't think.

Focus, Sarah.

The room was getting smaller, starting to spin.

Just breathe.

She gripped the edges of the washbasin to steady herself.

One breath at a time.

The wobbling was starting in her knees.

You can stop this.

She knew she could. It was only a panic attack. Mind over matter. She was in control. In control… Sarah held her breath for a moment, then let it out and turned to focus to the face in the mirror, and to the small abrasion on her left cheek. It was red, but not bleeding. Nothing too deep, nothing that mattered. Neither was the tiny cut along her right jaw. Insignificant again. Especially when she thought about Delroy, and all his injuries.

Besides the major ones, he'd been a mass of cuts and scrapes, some that would, no doubt, leave scars. And then there were the emotional scars. He had so much trauma to overcome, so much recovery ahead of him. Perhaps she would try and get his address so she could check in on him from time to time, just to see how he was doing. Not as a doctor, but as…as someone who'd shared an experience with him.

Cleaning herself up to where she was presentable took Sarah nearly ten minutes, dabbing gingerly at all the spots that were now becoming sore. But after they were clean, and after she'd made the assessment that everything was super-ficial, she took one final look in the mirror, hoping she could hold everything together until she was back in her cabin. These panic attacks…she hated them. They made her look weak, feel weak. Feel out of control. And for someone who'd owned an immediate care center, which had depended on her always being in control not just for herself but for everyone working for her, she absolutely despised what she'd become.

That face in the mirror…she hardly even recognized it any more. Didn't want to recognize it.

Disgusted with herself on many levels, Sarah put on the clothes Clarice had left on a chair outside the bathroom. Admittedly, now that she was clean again, she did feel a little better. But the clothes Clarice had chosen for her…hot pink *short* shorts, with much less fabric in them than anything she'd ever worn in public, with the exception of a swimsuit. And the top…pink and blue floral, bright colors, in a stretchy knit fabric—much less fabric than the shorts—that left nothing to the imagination about her breasts, now that her torn bra was in the trash can. Clarice's idea of a shirt pulled tight across Sarah, showing off the precise outlines of her nipples, and it didn't come within a good hand's width of covering her belly button, it was so short.

"Well," she said, assessing herself in the mirror, not sure she wanted to walk back through town to the ship dressed *this* way. But what other choice did she have, other than her own clothes, which were filthy, and in shreds? Probably discarded already, as Clarice had carried them off the second Sarah had handed them out the door in exchange for what she had on now. Which turned out to be the case she found out once she'd stepped out of the bathroom. Her old clothes, bra included, were already in the incinerator.

"You look beautiful," Clarice said, smiling her approval at the way Sarah wore the outfit.

"It's a little…small, don't you think?" She tried tugging down on the shirt but all that did was reveal more breast.

"But you can wear small. Better than me. I've lost so much weight these past months, worrying about Lachelle the way I've been doing, that my clothes practically hang on me."

Well, nothing about this outfit was hanging on her. Sarah took another look down at herself, and decided to make the best of it. "You have a daughter?" she asked.

"She's out with Dr Mike right now. He's supposed to be

examining her, but they play more than anything else, when he comes to look at her leg."

"He makes houses call?" That seemed odd.

"Every time the ship docks here. He keeps an eye on Lachelle's progress, especially now, with her growing so much. She's wearing a new one and he wants to make sure it fits her properly."

Sarah didn't follow that. "A new what?"

Clarice looked surprised by the question." A new leg," she said, like Sarah should have known. "My Lachelle has to have a new leg made for her when she has a growth spurt, then Dr Mike comes to check, to make sure the fit is good and that Lachelle is working with it properly. I trust him more than I do the public clinic here."

So, the child had a prosthetic leg. And Michael had been on his way to visit her, which was why he'd carried his medical bag with him. She'd wondered why he'd happened to have it but that explained a lot. He was making a house call of sorts, and lucky for her he was. Lucky for Delroy, too. "How old is Lachelle?" Sarah asked, on her way to the bedroom door.

"Ten. Eleven in two months. Big girl for her age. Looks more like fourteen, she's been developing so fast."

Such a rough age, growing up. Almost into adolescence, all those hormonal changes going on. And a prosthesis to contend with. Her heart went out to the child. "But she gets along well with it…with her new leg?" She asked that, rather than asking if Lachelle had other disabilities.

"She gets along beautifully. Better than I would if I'd had the accident and ended up the way she did. She's good in school, she plays with her friends, rides a bicycle. Dr Mike introduced us to a very good man who specializes in prosthetics for children, and that has been a blessing for us because he knows just what Lachelle needs."

Once Sarah had stepped out into the hall, she immediately heard the giggling of a young girl. And deeper, more resonant laughing she took to be Michael's. It was interesting that the ship's doctor had one special patient here in Nassau, but as it was really none of her business, she wouldn't ask how that came to be. Even though she wanted to.

"Delroy went straight to surgery," Michael reported, once Sarah stepped into the living room. "No word yet on how he's doing other than he's still holding on well. Not conscious, but they said that his vital signs were much improved."

"He's my friend," Lachelle piped up. "We go to school together, and play together."

"Do you like him better than me?" Michael asked, the corners of his mouth turning down to feign hurt.

Lachelle giggled. "He's here all the time. You're not. So I have to like him better when he's here. But I like you better now, and every time you come to visit me because you bring me candy."

"So now I understand," Michael said. "You're fickle. Do you know what that means?"

Lachelle looked puzzled for a moment, then her face brightened. "It means I can like Delroy better when he's here, and I can like you better when you're here."

"But what if we're both here together?" Michael asked. "Then what would you do?"

"I'd like whoever's closest to me the best," Lachelle said, with perfect ten-year-old logic. "Especially if he has candy."

Michael was seated on a wooden chair and Lachelle was standing across the room from him, smiling for all she was worth. She was a beautiful child. Smooth black skin. Black hair, dark brown eyes and a smile that could have melted even the coldest heart. It gave Sarah a little tug, thinking about how she'd wanted children, first when she'd been married to Kerry, then again when she'd been engaged to Cameron. She was almost thirty-five now, and while the longing hadn't gone away, the expectation had. "And what if I'm the one who's closest to you?" she asked Lachelle.

"I might like you best, but I don't even know you." She looked Sarah over, head to toe. "But you *are* wearing my mama's clothes, so I suppose I *could* like you, too."

"Well, I'm Sarah," Sarah said.

"And you're a doctor, like Dr Mike," Lachelle said, quite matter-of-factly. "I'm going to be a doctor, too. An orthopedic surgeon. Dr Mike says that when the time comes, he'll help me find the best medical school."

It crossed Sarah's mind that Michael and Clarice might be involved, as there was no sign of a permanent man in this house. Not here in this room, not in the bedroom either. Michael certainly did seem like he had an important place in this family, though, especially with the way Lachelle seemed to adore him. "Well, I'm sure he'll have some very good suggestions."

"And I'll work with children like me, who have had amputations. And like Dr Mike."

That's right. Michael was a surgeon. She'd forgotten all about that. "I think you'll make a fine surgeon," Sarah said, as she watched Lachelle walk cross the room. She was in shorts, not at all self-conscious about showing off her prosthetic leg. It came over the knee and stopped at mid-thigh. Not the old, clunky kind that imitated the real thing, but a lightweight metal variety that showed it for what it was…an artificial limb. A functional part of the body meant to work, not look like it was real. The newer ones were easier, had more precision to them. While she wasn't an expert in the field, she'd done enough reading to know that technology had come a long way these past few years and the science involved in making a leg or an arm was as close to being exact as you could get. Anyone wearing one could expect high function, and high function seemed to be the case with Lachelle, because her limp was barely noticeable as she moved with all the agility of any ten-year-old. She seemed quite athletic, in fact.

"Fritters, Dr Mike?" Clarice called from the hallway. "Or a salad this time?"

"Why do you even bother to ask?" he asked, standing up.

"And what will you have?" Clarice asked Sarah.

"Excuse me?"

"Conch fritter? Conch salad? Conch chowder? We have conch just about any way it can be eaten, and if you know of a better way than I have to fix it, tell me and I'll fix that."

"Conch?" Sarah whispered to Michael. "What's conch?"

"Shellfish. You know, the big shell you can hold up to your ear and hear the ocean in it? That's a conch shell."

"Cannot," Lachelle said.

"Can too," Michael argued.

"Cannot," Lachelle said again.

"You go bring me a conch shell and I'll show you how you can hear the ocean in it." It was an old myth, but a fun one.

With that, Lachelle took him up on the challenge and went running out of the room. Sarah watched, amazed by her speed down the hall. With a pair of long pants on, no one would even know she'd had an amputation.

"So, what kind of conch do you want?" Michael prompted, taking Sarah by the arm and leading her down the hall that went into the back door of the little café.

Once inside, she did have to admit that it smelled wonderful. And she was actually hungry. Crawling under that jitney had worked up quite an appetite in her. "What are my choices again?"

In the end, she settled on the fritters—little pieces of conch dipped into batter and fried, then served with a spicy sauce. Good choice, she discovered after the first bite. "It's amazing," she said, sitting across from Michael at a little table in the kitchen, one used by the cooks and servers when they wanted to take a break. The dining area was full, and a line of people waiting to get in spread all the way down the sidewalk. That's what made this private little dining nook work out perfectly for them. "I had no idea there was such a thing as conch."

"It's one of my favorite parts of the cruise, even though it's not served on the ship."

"That, and sitting alone in a karaoke bar," she commented, as a drop of the dipping sauce dribbled down her fingers and she unconsciously licked it off. "Funny, how we keep turning up in the same places, isn't it?"

"Maybe I *am* following you," he teased. "Maybe it's not a coincidence after all."

"If you are, you must be disappointed with what you're seeing, because I'm not at all an interesting person. I keep to myself and don't get involved in much of anything. I don't sing karaoke in the lounge, don't mingle with the people on the ship, don't get wrapped up in the group tours off the ship. Meaning I'd think you could find someone better to follow than me."

"Actually, I think you're interesting. The fact that you're a doctor has caught my interest, anyway. And keeping that little bit of information from me when I was treating you is even more interesting. Of course, I can't ask you about that, can I?" He arched a playful eyebrow.

That was a definite hint, but she wasn't going for it. She liked Michael well enough, even felt oddly attracted to him—likely because they shared the same profession—but that didn't call for some kind of revelation, where she laid out the details of her husband's death and her fiancé's cancer, then explained that she'd quit medicine because as a doctor she'd realized how very little she could do, even when it had been for someone she'd loved at the time they'd most needed her. That she was a failure in the things that mattered,. No, that was none of Michael's business, so she avoided the conversation altogether. "I collected stamps when I was a little girl, but I didn't tell you about that either," she said. "People are entitled to their privacy, Michael, and your knowing that I was a junior philatelist is private."

"Is that why you didn't ask about Lachelle? You're respecting her privacy?"

"If I ask questions, then I have to answer questions. And I don't want to answer questions, so I don't ask."

"Well, it keeps things simple that way, doesn't it?"

Rather than nodding, she stuck another piece of conch in her mouth and chewed.

"Car accident. Her father was driving, and they were hit by someone driving a truck. Her father was killed immediately, and Lachelle was thrown clear, but her leg couldn't be saved. They tried for months. She had several surgeries, but the infection got the better of her. She was brave about it, though. Very pragmatic for someone so young, but you've seen how she is…brighter than most children her age. And very well adjusted."

Better adjusted than most adults, too, Sarah thought. "So, you and Clarice…" she started to ask, but stopped. She didn't ask, she didn't answer. Although she was interested in the relationship.

"We're not involved romantically, if that's what you were going to ask. Not Clarice and me. Not me and anybody. And in the spirit of being mysterious or stubborn, let's just say that I don't do it, I don't talk about it and I don't answer questions about it either." He paused for a moment, then frowned. "Where have I heard that before?"

"OK, I get it. And just so you'll know, I wasn't curious about your relationships," she lied. In truth, she was, but they'd established their lines now. No crossing over them. "I was just curious how you two met, and how you came to be a consultant for her daughter. Since you're on the ship, it seems it might have been difficult for you to find the time."

"In case you hadn't noticed, that's a doctor question. But you're the one who won't answer doctor questions, aren't you, so that makes me the one who does."

His teasing was downright sexy. This was a man who had the power to distract her in ways she probably didn't even know about. "You don't have to answer anything. In fact, we can have a mutual understanding that we discuss weather and the ship's shuffleboard game, and nothing else."

"Except I like to answer doctor questions."

"Unlike me," she said. Michael wasn't subtle in the least, and he didn't even try hiding the fact. But she was curious about what he *was* hiding. Unfortunately, she couldn't ask.

"You said it. I didn't. And just for the record, Lachelle and I met in a clinic in the States. One for amputees."

That made sense. He the doctor, she the patient. Sarah was glad for the girl because Michael seemed to be a compassionate man. "I'm glad it was you there with me today," she said. "Even when I was practicing medicine, that kind of rescue wasn't at all like anything I'd ever done, so when I found out that the person helping me was you…you don't know how happy I was to have you there. I was scared to death, and there's nothing mysterious or stubborn about that."

"Well, to be honest, I'd much rather be treating a good case of heartburn than driving a bus with two people underneath. But if me being there made you feel better, I'm glad I was."

"You did a good job, Michael. I think that if you ever decide to give up medicine you might find another career in driving a jitney," she teased, even though her hands were shaking again as she thought about what had happened. This was pleasant though, eating informally here in the kitchen with someone she really did find herself liking more and more all the time.

"So, what career do you find yourself in now that you've given up medicine? And for the record, that's not a doctor question. It's more about lifestyle, and you didn't put that on the taboo list."

"Maybe it's not specifically a doctor question, but it's getting awfully close to the edge."

"Close, but not over."

She stared at him for a moment, the expression on her face giving away nothing. "I'll concede you the point. Just this once."

"Just this once?"

He cocked a playful eyebrow. And infuriatingly, playful eyebrow. The gesture was pure sex, filled with all the innuendoes something so simple could be, and it was all she could do to drag out the answer. "I, um…I have no career at the moment. I'm just…I'm just living life as it comes." He knew exactly what he was doing to her, taking pleasure in it, damn him. "Going on holiday, seeing the sights." To avoid the spell he seemed to be putting over her, she stared intently into the dipping sauce. "No real plans yet, which is fine because living day to day is all the challenge I want. I have the money, and the time, so why not?" She instantly regretted giving him so much insight into her life, but Michael was so easy to talk that her talk turned into babbling.

"I'm a little surprised by that. You don't seem like the kind woman who'd want to be idle for very long."

She dragged another conch fritter through the dipping sauce, then debated whether or not she could eat another bite. Rather than deciding, she simply held onto it for a minute. "I'm not idle so much as I'm doing all the things people promise themselves they'll do once they retire and never get around to doing for whatever reason. I just decided to take an early retirement and start on my list now, rather than later." Not a good explanation, but it would do. And true to her fashion, it skirted the truth.

To keep from answering another of his questions, she popped the conch into her mouth, instantly regretting it as she was so full already. But she forced herself to chew, then swallow. Then she stood. "Look, I think I'm going to head back to the ship now. I know we've got another three hours in port, but I'm not really in the mood to be a tourist any more today."

"I'll go with you," he offered, dropping his napkin to the table and standing up, too.

"You don't have to. I'm sure Lachelle would love to spend

more time with you. And maybe you see other patients here…"

"Lachelle is out playing with her friends, and I have no more patients."

She wanted to ask if he and Clarice might like some time alone, in spite of his denials of a romantic relationship with her, or anybody else, but out of respect for his personal boundaries she didn't. "You don't have to babysit me. I'll be fine. No more crawling under jitneys unless absolutely necessary."

"I have duty in an hour," he said, heading over to where Clarice was giving instructions to one of the cooks. "So we may as well walk back together. And with the way that outfit looks on you, you probably need a male escort to protect you."

He eyed her up and down, not in the clinical way a doctor would but in the way a very appreciative, very hungry man might. Like the man he would protect her from on the street. None of that was lost on her, and she did have the decency to blush. But Michael didn't see that as he was busy giving Clarice a very circumspect kiss on the cheek. Definitely not the kiss of a lover.

For some strange reason Sarah felt better about that. But it did make her wonder, because a man like Michael shouldn't have sworn off that kind of relationship the way he'd claimed he had.

Sarah said her farewells to Clarice, then to Lachelle, who was in the yard when she and Michael stepped outside. "You coming back with Dr Mike next time?" the girl asked, as she hugged Michael around the waist and pretended she wasn't going to let him go.

"I wish I could, but I've got someplace else to go after this cruise." She wasn't sure where. The truth was, she hadn't made any plans. Not in a very long time. Something would come to her, however. It always did. "But the next time I'm in Nassau, I'll be sure to come see you." She had no plans to return to Nassau, but she could. Living the way she did, there was nothing to stop her.

After walking a few blocks, dodging the blatant comments from strangers about the way she looked—mighty hot mama, they were calling her—and shrinking from the blazing stares, Sarah and Michael finally retreated to the relative privacy of a cab for the rest of their journey back to the ship. But in the cab, an old rattletrap of a car that smelled of human bodies and tobacco and had badly ripped seats, she and Michael barely spoke, which was odd as the condition of the seat practically forced her into his lap, they had to sit so close to each other. Good thing she'd had a quick bath, she thought as her shoulder wedged into his arm.

"So, have you ever been to the Bahamas before?" he finally asked, as it became apparent they were stuck in a traffic jam, going nowhere any time soon.

"No. Never been on a cruise, never been to the Bahamas." Stiff conversation. *Very stiff.*

Another minute passed before he spoke again. "If you don't consider it private, could I ask where you're from?"

"Chicago, born and raised." She might have asked him the same, but at that moment the cab lurched forward several car lengths, then stopped again. "Do I make you nervous?" she asked impulsively.

He bent to her ear. "You don't but your clothes do."

She glanced down, shocked by what she saw. Her short shorts had crept up as far as they could go. Likewise her shirt. In attempting to get settled in the back of the cab, apparently her clothing had…shifted. Indecently so. "You're a doctor," she whispered back, trying to force her clothes back into the right position as the cab driver glanced in his rear-view mirror to see what all the whispering was about. "This shouldn't disturb you."

"I'm not on duty. I'm allowed to be disturbed."

That was kind of cute, actually. And she was flattered. Not

so much that she'd ever wear these clothes again, though. Or anything like them. But after being so long without a man, it was nice knowing that she still did have the power to attract one. Too bad she didn't want one. But one year married to one man, then a year and a half engaged to another…the third time wasn't going to be the charm. She simply wouldn't let that happen.

"I thought I might find you here," Michael said, sliding into the seat next to her. The same dark corner of the same karaoke lounge. Tonight the singer wasn't so loud or off key. And a few more people had found this hidden little gem, so they didn't have most of the place to themselves like before. But Sarah'd been there an hour, in her regular out-of-the-way booth, sipping ginger ale and wondering if he might meander in.

"It's as good a place as any to spend time," she said, watching the waitress take note of Michael. She literally perked up, primped her hair a little, tugged the neckline of her black blouse a little lower and undid an extra button. It was clear that Michael could have his pick of them if he wanted. For a moment she almost regretted the boundaries she'd established, because she sure wanted to ask him why he didn't want his pick. Especially with a waitress who was doing everything she could, except make an announcement over the karaoke machine, to attract Michael's attention.

"Not really," he said, as he gestured her over to the table. "But it's a habit that won't get you into trouble."

Oh, I see trouble, Sarah thought as the waitress slithered her way up to the table.

"The usual, Doctor?" Heidi asked. She was almost breathless, and it wasn't from over-exertion.

"I'm not in the mood for a Cubano tonight. Just bring me a diet soda and a basket of pretzels." Heidi looked almost crestfallen as she scampered away, like she took Michael's change in order personally.

"That's not a proper meal," Sarah said, trying to sound light about it. "After all the lectures you've given me on the subject of proper dietary habits…"

"Do you always listen to what the doctor says?" he asked, relaxing into the booth. "Because you don't seem like the type."

"Depends on the doctor. I've known a few whose word I'd take as gospel, and a few I wouldn't trust as far as I could throw them."

"So, when the pretzels arrive, if I were to tell you that they are a perfectly balanced meal, lots of vitamins, good nutrition, would you take my word for it?"

Sarah didn't even hesitate. "I'd take your word, Michael. I may not practice as a doctor any longer, but I'm still a pretty good judge of one." The next thing out of her mouth would have been something about why such a good doctor was limiting himself to a ship's practice, but Heidi plunked down the basket of pretzels at that moment and Sarah shoved one in her mouth before she asked a question that would, on some level, involve her with Michael in something more than a casual chat in a dark little karaoke lounge.

"Delroy's in Intensive Care," he said, picking up a pretzel, studying it for a moment then dropping it back into the basket with a weary sigh. "They removed his spleen, surgically repaired his arm, splinted his broken leg, stitched up numerous cuts. He has a concussion, but he's beginning to stir so they don't anticipate permanent brain damage. Oh, and they discovered four broken ribs. His surgeon told me that one was so badly separated that if Delroy had been dragged out from under the bus, the rib would have gone right though his lung, and he'd probably have died on the spot, owing to all the other injuries and blood loss. You had a good instinct with that one, Sarah. You saved the boy's life."

"That's good."

Michael didn't answer for a minute, and when he finally

did, he seemed almost angry. "Did you hear what I said? I just told you that you saved the boy's life, yet you seemed…unaffected. I don't understand that. I'm emotionally drained, and I wasn't under that bus. You were, and you're so…"

"Uninvolved," she said, trying to sound detached and dispassionate when, in fact, she was so elated that Delroy would recover that what she really wanted to do was grab Michael, hug him, kiss him. But what she was putting on for him now was part of the facade, and she was good at it. Well practiced. "I did what anybody would have done, but that doesn't give me any kind of a bond to the boy. I'm glad he's going to be fine, and that's all there is to it." Except the part of her that wanted to get up on the table and dance. That's the way she used to be, though. Good news for the patient became her own good news. Bad news, and she suffered right along with them.

But not any more. Sarah Collins, retired doctor, forced herself to stay uninvolved.

"I don't believe that," he said. "I was there this afternoon. Remember? I saw you under the bus, saw the way you held onto that child and protected him. Saw the way you wouldn't leave him even when your own life might have been in danger. So you can tell me you're uninvolved all you want, but those are words, Sarah, that I wouldn't trust as far as I could throw them."

"Why does it matter to you?" she snapped, as she started to scoot around to the other side of the booth. It was time to leave. Time to retire to her cabin and figure out what she was going to do. Stay, or leave the ship? Michael was becoming too personal, and if she wasn't careful, she'd get personal right back at him. She was seriously considering it. He was more tempting than anything in a long, long time and that's what scared her, because part of her really wanted to give in to the temptation. A big part of her did, anyway. "Why do you even care what I do, or how I feel? If I say that I'm not involved with Delroy, who are you to question me…no, accuse me of lying about it?"

Michael grabbed her by the arm before she could scoot to the other side of the circular booth. "I'm not sure who I am, Sarah. Not sure why I care. But I do."

She wrenched free. "Well, don't. People who care for me end up…" She didn't finish her sentence. Instead, she got up and walked away. Just like she always did now.

CHAPTER FIVE

SARAH stared up at the row of coconut palms on the hill above the fruit plantation. She was totally isolated from the other cruise passengers who'd come ashore here in Jamaica. That was by design, of course. While people were running off to go rafting and bird watching, she'd decided to wander off on her own and stay away from the main flurry. Theirs wasn't the only ship in dock at the moment, and there were tourists everywhere, but she never considered herself a true tourist, so traveling along the dusty roads by taxi to destinations no one else cared to see suited her just fine.

The ship would be there for twelve hours to give its passengers an opportunity to experience Montego Bay both during the day and at night, when it came alive in ways only Jamaica could come alive. But by the time evening rolled around she intended to be back on ship and, truth be told, the only reason she'd come ashore had been that twelve hours in dock seemed like such a long time. She wanted to avoid Michael, and that would be hard to do on a practically empty ship, as they kept bumping into each other on a full ship.

The ride was jarring as there were giant potholes in the road, but Sarah barely noticed as her attention wasn't on where she was going. The taxi driver, a friendly man named Frank, was trying frantically to engage her in some way, talking incessantly about the countryside as they bumped their way from place to place, and she responded politely in the places that called for a response, although she just wasn't in the mood. So after two long hours of a tour she wasn't interested in, she asked Frank to drive her back to the ship, where she paid him a generous tip and went back to her cabin.

What was the nature of her latest discontent? The list was getting longer, she feared, and Michael had taken his place on it. Maybe at the top of it.

Two hours after her return to the ship, two hours of fretting and pacing the confined space of her cabin, always on the verge of a panic attack, Sarah decided to go out in search of a bite to eat. Something, anything, to get her out of that cramped space. Her first thought was the karaoke bar. Michael would be on duty so she wouldn't bump into him there, and at this late hour of the afternoon no one would be singing. So it would be a perfect place to be alone. Yes, perfect, she thought as she hurried down the corridor to the elevator.

After she punched the button, she stared at the floor, folded her arms across her chest and waited several seconds, until the doors parted. When she looked up, Michael standing in the center of the elevator, grinning at her. "Margueritaville," he said. One simple word and nothing else.

"Isn't Margaritaville a song?"

"It is, but I said Mar-*guer*-itaville, not Mar-*gar*-itaville." He gestured her into the elevator, but she stepped backwards as the doors started to close. Undaunted, he punched the "open" button, then wedged himself against the right door so it wouldn't close again. "I heard you'd come back early."

"I saw everything I wanted to see," she said. Everything she could see, with her thoughts so scattered. She was restless, and the reason was standing directly in front of her, looking so handsome she wanted to melt into his arms like she had that first day, only this time doing it on purpose. "One place is pretty much like another, and I did exactly what I wanted to do."

"Well, you ought to take a look at your face because, judging from the expression there, you haven't done anything you wanted to do in a long time."

"Why me, Michael? Why do you keep coming after me?"

As the elevator alarm started to sound, he stepped off. "I'm not coming after you, Sarah. But it's a pity that you isolate yourself so much you can't accept a simple gesture of friendship when it's offered."

"Is that what this is? A simple gesture of friendship? Because you've got hundreds of other people on the cruise who are probably clamoring to be your friend, and I'm the one who's not. Yet here you are, forcing something on me that I simply don't want."

Rather than being put off by that, as she'd expected he would be, he stepped even closer to her. So close she could smell the slight muskiness of his aftershave. "Your shell isn't as hard as you think it is, Sarah. I'm a student of human nature, and as you're saying one thing, your eyes are saying something entirely different."

She snapped her head up, glaring at him. "So, what is it you want from me, Michael? Sex? Is that what this is about? I'm the lady you've chosen to fulfill your needs on this particular cruise? Or maybe I'm the challenge you've picked to conquer? Are you taking bets on the outcome? Because if that's the case, how about we go back to my cabin, then you can strip me, throw me down on the bed and do whatever you want to satisfy that urge, or win that bet, and we can move on from there? You can go find your next conquest and I can do what I came on this cruise to do."

Anger sparked in Michael's dark eyes, but just for a second before his usual genial expression returned. "Apparently, I have a higher opinion of you than you have of yourself. Which is a pity, Sarah, because it's got to be miserable living the way you do, always pushing people away. Especially since that's going against your true nature."

She straightened her shoulders, still trying to hang onto her defiance, even though it was beginning to slip away. "You don't know a thing about my true nature."

"I know you've called to check on Delroy several times. That tells me something about you."

"You don't think I have the right to be concerned?" she snapped.

"The Sarah you're trying to be wouldn't be concerned. The Sarah I think you are would be. So you tell me, am I close to your true nature?"

This was crazy! She didn't have to argue with him. Didn't even have to speak to him, yet here she was, standing in a deserted corridor, pulse rate rising, breath coming shorter and shorter, nipples probably hardening, all because Michael made her respond in ways she'd thought dead a long time ago. She hadn't been with a man since Cameron, hadn't dated, hadn't kissed, hadn't even been alone with a man, and she did recognize her starving biological urges. Especially in her crazy responses to Michael. But that's all they were. Urges. She could control them.

She hoped.

"My true nature, Michael, is what I want it to be. It's whatever suits me at the moment."

A wicked little grin played across his face, on his lips, in his eyes. "So when you invited me to your cabin to let me throw you down on the bed and strip you naked, was that your true nature? At least, true for that moment?"

"You'd be disappointed in my true nature," she said flatly, trying to avoid the way he was baiting her now. It wasn't a sexual thing, but he was trying to goad her into something, and she didn't want to be goaded.

"I hardly think so, Sarah. But that's not why I came looking for you."

So this really wasn't an accidental encounter. Her heart did skip a beat knowing that, which was why she had to fight even harder now to keep herself under control. "Whatever it is, you shouldn't have," she said stiffly. "And just so you'll know, I don't date, don't get involved with men—"

"You think that's *not* obvious?" He chuckled. "You wear it like a banner. It's on your face, in the way you hold your body, the way you pull back even from people passing by you who are paying no attention to you whatsoever. Look, Sarah, I can respect the distance you want. I don't know what caused it and I'm not going to ask because I do believe that people have the right to be the way they want to be."

"And in your opinion, I'm being miserable. Is that it?" she snapped.

"Are you?" Before she could respond to that, he thrust out his hand to stop her. "No, don't answer that. It's none of my business."

She studied him for a moment, not sure what to make of this little quibble between them. It wasn't so much that they were arguing as establishing their ground rules. But for what? And for some reason, she didn't believe the boundaries being imposed were all about her. Michael kept his distance, too. His boundaries were as obvious to her as hers were to him. Which made this safe. So, maybe that was good. She liked him, and at another time in her life would probably have gotten involved with him.

For now, though, two people with strong boundaries worked. It broke up the monotony in her life, gave her that medical connection she still hungered for, and there was the added bonus of his company. She enjoyed it. Sexual attraction had definitely been in short supply in her life lately, and she did recognize it for what it was.

In other words, this alliance was safe, and safety was all she really wanted. "Tell me again why you came looking for me?"

"Margueritaville," he stated, like he had the first time. "I thought you might like to go there with me."

"Aren't you working?"

"I'm off duty for the next eight hours, and there's this nice cantina I try to get to here whenever I have the time. Good food, great music. And just so you won't consider this a date, I'll be going there even if you don't." A wide grin spread across his face. "And we'll take separate taxis, if that appeases your need to keep this casual."

How could any one man be so infuriating in one breath and so absolutely irresistible in the next? Even though she'd never heard of the place, all she wanted to do now was go to Margueritaville with Michael. In fact, she wanted it so badly it was like this was the only thing she'd ever wanted to do. "How about we take one taxi, and split the fare?"

"If you pay the taxi driver's tip," he said, still grinning, but more with his eyes now. Which caused goose-bumps to go wild up and down her arms.

"Both ways?" she asked, trying to keep a straight face, because his smile bought out a smile in her. "Because that doesn't seem fair to me."

"Sounds like we've got something to argue about in the taxi, doesn't it?" he said, then spun around and punched the elevator button. "I'll meet you on the dock in fifteen minutes." There were no gallantries after that. Michael merely stepped into the elevator and engaged himself in chat with a young couple who were clinging to each other so tightly it made Sarah think they might be honeymooners. He didn't look at her as the doors started to close, didn't acknowledge her in any way. Professional demeanor, she thought as she stood there, watching him, even doing some bold-faced admiring that he could see if he looked at her. Then, in the very last instant before the doors came together. Did he actually wink at her?

Margueritaville turned out to be a pleasant town sitting

right on the coastline. It was nearly dark when they arrived, but lights twinkled from every window along the street they traveled, giving the place a nice, welcoming feeling. It was congested, though, with tourists making their way down the coast to see the little town with the name that so closely resembled the popular song. "So which came first," she asked Michael, "the town, or the song?"

"The town, by a long stretch, and they're enjoying the popularity of their name now."

"How did you find it? By the name, like everybody else does?"

Michael leaned forward on the seat and gave the taxi driver instructions to turn at the next corner. They did, straight into a dark little alley. "Marguerite is my mother's name. I saw it on the map first time I came down here, and when I had the chance, I came here to have a look."

Halfway down the alley, Michael tapped the driver on the shoulder, and the cab came to a stop under a single light jutting out from the wooden building. True to their agreement, he paid his half of the fare, then jumped out of the cab, leaving Sarah to pay her half, as well as the driver's tip. Although, in his defense, he did go around and open the taxi door for her. But rather than offering her a hand as she climbed out, he stood back. More distance, she thought, and she wondered if that was on account of her wish to keep up the boundaries or his.

"Why are we going in the back way?" she asked, following him to the door.

"Less crowded."

"Like your booth in the karaoke bar?"

"You mean the booth you choose for yourself when you can beat me to it?"

He held the door open for her as she passed by him. Once inside, she ran straight into the wall, it was so dark in the corridor. "Don't they use lights in here?" she asked, backing away from the wall and thrusting out her hand to locate where she was and which way to go. But what she encountered, rather than another wall or obstacle, was Michael's chest. Strong, muscular, her palm flat on his chest, she drew in a ragged breath, but didn't remove her hand. Instead, she kept it there as his chest rose and fell with a breath. Then another breath. Then another.

Finally, she pulled back, but before she could pull back from him more than an inch or two he took hold of her wrist, and she was overcome with a rush of sexual twinges like she'd never felt in her life. Not with anybody.

All from an innocent touch in the dark!

Yet she made no move to pull away from him. Instead, she fought to keep her breathing steady as he pressed his way past her in the tight little hallway, pushing her back against the wall for that instant as their bodies met. And in that moment crazy, aroused thoughts ran through her mind... She wanted to, right there, like she'd never wanted to with any man in her life. Wanted to even more when she felt his hand skim up over her ribs and slide its way under the knit top she was wearing—the one Clarice had given her that she'd vowed never to wear again.

Sarah bit her lip to keep from sucking in a sharp, loud breath because she feared the least little sound would break this spell, and she didn't want it broken. Barriers were down, and she didn't know for how long. And while they were down she wanted everything from Michael that she could have.

Tilting her head to the side, she felt the nuzzle of his lips just at that tender spot where her neck and shoulder connected, and the liquid heat from something so simple melted down through to her very core, arousing her to the point that she pressed her hips against his, and felt his erection hard against her. She gasped, in spite of her resolve to be quiet, and that only intensified the pressure on her as he ground into her even harder.

Sarah was ready for him, in this dark little nook, even as her eyes were adjusting and she could see the outline of his body so close to her, pushing harder in such intimate ways. The feel of his fingers pushing away her bra to find her nipple, the feel of his lips on her jaw…

Somewhere in the distance the sound of shattering glass broke the mood, and Michael backed away from Sarah as quickly as Sarah adjusted her disheveled clothing. "Sounds like a tray of bar glasses," Michael said roughly, then cleared his throat. "Bet somebody's going to pay for that."

The liquid heat still flowing everywhere—through her breasts, between her legs, Sarah was able to answer only with a nod and something that amounted to a squeak. This was…incredible. Incredible and stupid! She was about to do, well…anything, everything, with Michael in the back hallway to a bar. That wasn't like her. She'd never been wild like that. Never been driven to the point of such extreme desire that it would compel her to do such an impulsive, crazy thing. Worst of all, the heat wasn't going away fast enough. She still wanted Michael. "Do they have tables here?" she asked, finally finding her voice. "Because I need a margarita in a big way. Two of them!"

Michael chuckled. "Can you imagine what would have happened if we didn't have boundaries?"

"I understand hormones and lust," she said stiffly.

"If that's what you want to call it." He took hold of her hand once more, but this time pulled her along the corridor until they entered the kitchen, where he greeted the cook, a man named Emilio, an assistant cook called Juan, and a large woman—not large in weight so much as stature—all decked out in multicolored scarves and large, jingling gold hoop earrings and bracelets. The woman had dark, smooth skin and bright eyes.

"I wondered when you'd be getting 'round to see me, man," she said to Michael. "I knew da boat was in, but I've been waiting all day to see the doc, and I was gettin' disappointed he wasn't comin'."

Michael dropped Sarah's hand and rushed over to give Evangeline, the proprietor of Evangeline's, a big hug. "Do you think I'd miss the chance for some of your jerk chicken?"

"You crave Evangeline's jerk chicken the way you should be craving a woman," Evangeline said, her jolly chuckle rolling out over the entire kitchen. Jerk chicken was a typically spicy Jamaican recipe, and a favorite of the locals as well as tourists. "The way you should be cravin' that one," she said, pointing to Sarah.

Sarah blushed, wondering if Evangeline had witnessed what had almost gone on in her back hall.

"You know you and your jerk chicken are the only things I've been craving tonight," Michael said, casting a sideways glance at Sarah. "And some good reggae music."

"You get the chicken and you get the good music, but you know you don't get Evangeline. I like my men…older. With lots of money. You're good-lookin', Doc, but I've got other needs you can't take care of." She cast a sly wink at Sarah. "But I'm guessin' what her needs are tonight, and it's not chicken and reggae."

Evangeline sauntered away, still laughing, while Sarah was coming to the decision to catch a cab and return to the ship. But Michael didn't give her an opportunity to slip back out the way they'd come in. As if he'd guessed what she might be planning, he grabbed her by the hand and pulled her the rest of the way through the kitchen into a dim room full of people, all sitting at tables or at the bar on the other side of the room—a bar backlit in blue. The place was packed, there was barely room to squeeze through as a saxophone wailed something so rhythmic on stage that most of the people in the club were clapping and stomping along to the music.

"How are we going to find a place to sit?" she shouted over

the music. Deep down, she really hoped they wouldn't find
a seat so they could leave. Or they'd find only one seat, for
Michael, so she could leave by herself. As it turned out,
Michael had a cozy little booth reserved for him, back in a
secluded corner, of course. They'd no sooner squeezed into
it when Evangeline appeared at the table with two tall
glasses—one with a fruit juice concoction she placed in front
of Michael and one with something yellow for her.

Evangeline gave her a toothy grin as she passed the glass
over. "From what I saw of you in the kitchen, I think you'll
be needing this. It's Evangeline's specialty." She actually
tweaked Sarah's cheek before she walked away.

"That means she likes you," Michael said. Or, actually,
practically shouted as he was sitting on the other side of the
booth. "I remember the first time she tweaked my cheek…"
The rest of what he said washed away in the noise and, to be
honest, Sarah didn't really care. She was so uncomfortable
being there now, after what had almost happened, that she
was happy to turn her attention to Evangeline's drink and lose
herself in it. What had she been thinking, giving in that way?
Never mind that it was in a public place!

Well, it wouldn't happen again. And Michael's suggestions to take two taxis…that's exactly what she intended to
do. Take her own taxi back to the ship as soon as she finished
Evangeline's rather tasty rum extravaganza.

OK, so he'd screwed up. The moment, and the opportunity,
got the best of him, but it wasn't like anything had really
happened between them. To look at Sarah, though, someone
might have made assumptions about all kinds of things having
gone on in Evangeline's back hall. Sarah looked guilty, and
she wore that guilt even now, twenty minutes later. But, damn
it, it just wasn't that big a deal. They'd flirted a little. Well,
maybe flirt wasn't accurate. But they'd stopped. That's all that
counted.

Sarah was sitting across the table from him, and she hadn't looked up from her drink for the last ten minutes. Hadn't really drunk any of it either. So what the hell was he supposed to do now? This was supposed to be a nice evening out for her, something to relax her and help take her mind off what always seemed to be bothering her, but it wasn't working.

"Want some chicken?" he asked, shoving the plate across the table to her.

She looked up, giving him a blank stare.

"The chicken. You should try some," he said again, only this time louder, trying to cut through the noise all around them.

Judging from her expression, she still didn't hear him, though. Or didn't want to. Normally the noise level in there was a blessing. He always slipped in the back door like he'd done tonight, come to this booth and eaten his chicken. Alone. There was something to be said for being alone in a crowd. Of course, most of the time Evangeline never let him be entirely alone, even though tonight she was staying away. Deliberately, he guessed. And for some reason, even with Sarah sitting across from him, he'd never felt so alone here as he did right now. "The chicken," he shouted, then finally gave up and scooted around to the other side of the circular booth. Surprisingly, she didn't push herself away from him, but she did cringe when his arm brushed against hers. "Look," he said, bending toward her, yet taking particular caution not to touch her. "I'm sorry about what happened."

It was an opening, and he waited for her to respond, but all she did was give him a stiff nod. Well, so much for trying to approach her. One little lapse in good sense had ruined her evening which, in turn, was ruining his as he'd truly thought she might enjoy this. So maybe they should simply return to the ship and promise to avoid each other for the rest of the cruise. Or perhaps he should send her back in a cab, alone, while he stayed and enjoyed the routine he'd established over the months—jerk chicken, reggae and a pleasant way to relax.

"Do you want to go back to the ship?" he asked. "Since that little faux pas in the hall is bound to ruin at least one of our evenings, maybe you'd be more comfortable having yours ruined somewhere else." OK, so that was harsh but, damn it, he was trying to make up for his mistake and she wasn't giving him an inch. So why keep trying? "How about I just call you a cab, and we'll pretend it never happened?"

"Pretend it never happened?" she sputtered, finally turning sideways to look at him. "How can you pretend something like that never happened?"

The way the dim light overhead caught the glint of her hair, the angry spark of what had to be the most beautiful eyes he'd ever seen... Honestly, he wasn't the least bit sorry about what had almost happened. If the truth be told, he'd been aroused to the point that he'd have probably pushed her into the little broom closet just inside Evangeline's back door and broken a promise he'd made himself nearly two years ago. "You can quit dwelling on it, then enjoy the food and the music, that's how."

"It's that simple for you?"

"Look, Sarah, what happened...happened. Apparently, we've got some pretty good chemistry going between us, and we let it get away from us for a couple of minutes. It happens. We're humans. Hormones flow. I've apologized, and I'll apologize again, but if you want to know my true feelings, I'm not really all that sorry. I enjoyed it and if the situation presented itself again, I'd probably do the same thing." Against his dictates, but not so much against his will. Sarah was the first woman who'd turned his head since his self-imposed ban on women and his whole relationship avoidance, and he didn't really object to his feelings toward her as strenuously as he should. Or wanted to. Probably because she put up enough barriers for both of them that he felt relatively safe with her. If he couldn't resist her, which it seemed he couldn't, at least she'd resist him. "But that's all I can do. Say I'm sorry and give you an option…to stay here with me and enjoy the evening or leave and do whatever you want to do."

He hoped she'd stay, but from the long pause he was pretty sure she wouldn't.

After nearly a minute, Sarah finally spoke. "It wasn't just you," she said so quietly he had to lean in close to hear her. "I was ready to do something I've never done before, in such a public place. And I'm not like that, Michael. But for a minute I forgot who I was and where I was…"

"And that's so bad?" he asked, for his sake as much as hers.

"I'd like to think that I have more control," she admitted.

"Have you ever just let yourself go, Sarah? Been spontaneous about anything?"

"I think the way I live *is* spontaneous," she said defensively. "You know, living for the moment, that kind of thing. That's me! That's all I do, living in the moment, going with the flow."

"Very rigidly," he argued. "You strike me as a woman who'd much rather make plans and live by the rules."

"Rules are made to be broken, and plans are a trap. My only rule is that I'm not allowed to make plans. Why bother? They don't work out. Trust me, I've lived that life before, and been disappointed by it. So why put myself through anything like it again?"

"Maybe you're right. Why put yourself through it?" Broken plans only caused pain, and he'd had his share. Sarah was right. Plans were a trap, which was why he'd avoided making them himself. Once was enough. In life, in love, he didn't make plans any more either. Not even in the short term.

Michael finally broke through the barrier between them, scooting so close to Sarah they were sitting hip to hip. "I've lived that life before, too. Tends to make you a bit cynical, I think."

"Ah, the man who knows."

"What I know is that you can plan your life down to the smallest details, live by that plan and count on it to be your beacon. As long as you're headed toward the light you're doing fine, things are going to work out. Then one little thing happens…" *Like having a leg blown off by a landmine and watching your buddies die beside you while you're helpless to do anything…* "And it all changes. Goes straight to hell. All your plans are gone, everything you've hoped and dreamed for vanished, and you suddenly find yourself in a position you can't even conceive of. Your meticulous life, the one you could picture in a panoramic view, isn't yours any more and you're left wondering what comes next. What the hell are you going to do now." Something he'd been wondering from the day the doctors had released him from rehab and sent him out into the world to face whatever it was he had to face. Eighteen months between the hospital and rehab, living in an altered reality, and he'd been totally unprepared for his new reality. Even after a year of living inside his new reality, he still wasn't prepared for it.

"You speak from experience," she said.

Michael cracked a bitter laugh. "We all have experiences that mold us, whether or not we want them, don't we?" Like a fiancée who had been repulsed by a less than perfect body in the man she'd supposedly to loved, one who hadn't even pretended to be sympathetic or unaffected when she'd seen him without his prosthesis. That had been an experience that truly had molded him, and not in a good way, for future relationships. It was another one of these things that fit into the category of why bother to put himself through it? He'd already seen the results. Didn't need to repeat them.

"Want them or plan for them. You know what they say about the best-laid plans…" She finally picked up a strip of the chicken and took a little nibble, caught off guard by the spicy heat of it. Coughing as she tried to swallow it, Michael shoved his fruit drink over to her, frowning as she took a greedy gulp. Yes, he did know about what happened to the best-laid plans. The problem was, he hadn't planned on Sarah. She was the sexiest woman he'd ever known in his life, and if he wasn't careful, some of his best-laid plans were in serious jeopardy of going astray.

Thinking about his current course as he picked up a strip of jerk chicken, Michael wondered if now wouldn't be a good time to actually form a plan...a plan to *not* get involved. He also wondered if he was drawn to Sarah because he was more like her than he cared to admit. In her, the sadness and isolation was so easy to see, but what he saw in her...was that what other people saw when they looked at him?

Sighing, Michael tossed the chicken strip back onto the plate then leaned back in his seat, still taking care not to accidentally brush Sarah's arm or bump her hip. Distance was best, and he was going to have to be very careful to keep his.

"I'm sorry I overreacted a while ago," she said, just when he was about to give in to the melancholy crashing down on them. "You're right. It's chemistry, and I shouldn't be such a prude about it, because under normal circumstances it's a good thing for most people. A wonderful thing. But in my life those kinds of things never happen."

"Because you don't allow them?" The way he didn't allow them any more?

"Honestly, yes. Keeping focused always seems to work best for me. There's no need for me to be any other way because what I am, what I do, suits me."

No, it didn't, and he could see that very plainly. Even now, as she toyed with another piece of chicken, licking a little of the spicy-hot marinade off it first, then licking her lips and letting her tongue wander across her bottom lip, he was as aroused as he'd been in the hallway. More so, because he could see her now, see all the sexy insinuations of her movements...insinuations she didn't even know she was making. Right at that very moment he wished he had some of her focus, because if he wasn't careful he'd find himself in the same position he'd been in earlier in the dark hall, and even he had only so much restraint he could call on to save himself. The best-laid plans were about to fail him.

But deep down didn't he want to fail in this one? Of course he did! He was a man, after all. And she was...well, everything he'd ever dreamed of in a woman. And, damn it, human nature did prevail, his disability and his checkered past notwithstanding. "I know you've got your resolve, but are you ever tempted, Sarah?" he asked, his voice much lower, much more seductive than he'd intended it to be. "Maybe you don't ever give in, but are you tempted to? I mean, like right now. After what happened in the hallway..."

She glanced into his eyes, very seriously. "Yes, I get tempted. You could have had me in the hall, Michael."

Well, that certainly wasn't what he'd expected from her. Wasn't what he'd needed either because in the next instant she was in his arms...whether he pulled her there or she'd gone voluntarily, he didn't know, but the temptation melted away all resolve as his lips crushed hers and he tasted the slight heat of the spice still lingering on her lips. The pull was too great to resist, even though he knew he should pull back and leave well enough alone. But what he knew and what he did were two different things as his tongue forced her lips apart, only to join with a tongue that was as eager as his to probe.

As he caressed her upper lip with his tongue, moving it in slow, delicious circles, she reached up to stroke his hair, running light fingers through it at first. Then as he nipped softly at her lip, she pulled with some vigor until he tilted his head back and away from her, but only enough to allow her to kiss his neck then his jaw. Sweet mercy, he'd never felt anything like it! The way her tongue played gently up his throat, over his jaw… The plan be damned. He'd deal with its demise later.

Once she reached his mouth, she was the one to do the probing this time, to run her tongue over his lips, to delve inside and once she'd found his tongue to suck it with a potent energy like no one had ever done to him before. And if he had been aroused before this, he was now aroused to the point that he was uncomfortable, and had this not been a public place they would have been past the point of no return. But this *was* a public place, a fact that niggled in the back of his mind as he returned a forceful kiss to Sarah, his full, open mouth taking hers in a greed he'd never before known as both her hands snaked around his neck and pulled him tightly to her, as tight as human beings could possibly be without being inside one another.

And as the kiss should have been diminishing, she arched herself back into the booth seat, pulling him along with her, causing him to shift to a position that was nearly on top of her. His arms wrapped around her as she turned sideways into a semi-straddle and her knee came up over his thigh. Because they were in a dark, secluded booth where the only people who could see them were the ones who wanted to, he pulled Sarah up over his lap until she was fully straddling him, looking down, pressing her hands to his cheeks and lowering her mouth over his. Tongues sought tongues again, nipping, probing…harder, faster, the urgency growing until Michael moaned the moan of a man who couldn't take it any more. He was at his limit, and so was Sarah as she pulled away, looked down at him with longing in her eyes like he'd never seen before, then slid off his lap.

Without a word she straightened her clothes, slipped out of the booth and left Evangeline's.

That evening, needless to say, they returned to the ship in separate taxis.

CHAPTER SIX

ONE more day, and they'd docked again. A good many people had gone ashore for various expeditions and shopping, spending their few hours milling about, but Sarah hadn't gotten off ship this time because there hadn't been anything she'd really wanted to do. Neither had Michael. She'd seen him in passing once since two nights ago in Evangeline's. He'd been strolling along the deck, pushing a patient in a wheelchair down to the cabana chairs, and he'd been so caught up in casual chat with the old man he probably hadn't even noticed her. Or hadn't wanted to. Whatever the case, the instant she'd seen him, she'd turned around and hurried off in another direction.

It wasn't like she was embarrassed, though. Because, oddly, she wasn't. What they'd done in the booth at Evangeline's had been the culmination of what they'd started earlier in the hallway, which had been the climax of some pretty pent-up feelings. She understood. And Michael was right about it, too. They did have chemistry going on between them. What was the point of denying it? And if he thought that she couldn't be spontaneous, well…he'd seen her at her spontaneous best that night.

Truly, it did surprise her that she'd acted that way. In the dozens of times she'd replayed that little scenario in her mind since then, she hadn't found an excuse for what she'd done other than she'd simply wanted to. *With Michael*. No one else had ever stirred that little wild streak in her like he had and she'd returned to the ship a very sexually frustrated woman. In her mind she'd had herself naked with him over and over—in her cabin bed, in the shower, the dark hallway at Evangeline's and even in the booth. In some of her fantasies they were even in their private little section on deck, behind the bar. And those kisses weren't bound by what was proper in public either.

Even thinking about that now was dangerous because it put her in a mood to be reckless, and if there was one thing she wasn't, it was reckless. She could be. Maybe she even wanted to be, but recklessness led to other things. A brief, sexually satisfying affair might have been just fine.

But she wasn't wired that way. She knew it. For her, anything less than full commitment with all the trimmings simply didn't work. Although, with her history, full commitment didn't work out so well either.

So, skipping any embarrassment that might have normally occurred at such wanton abandonment of everything she'd worked so slavishly to keep in order, it was best to hold Michael at a distance now. Put what they had into its proper perspective, rationalize it into what it was—a moment of lust—and let it go at that. Oh, and be grateful to know *that* part of her was still alive. She'd figured it was long dead. After Kerry, then Cameron, she'd wanted it to be dead. Willed it away to a dark, dusty corner, never to surface again.

Sarah was happy it had surfaced, however, because this was the first time she'd felt normal in so long. Now that she knew she was relatively fit in those ways, however, it was time to ignore it all again. Time to steady herself with a deep breath, hold her head up high, and get on with her life…whatever that was.

So now not only was she avoiding Michael, she was avoiding all their usual places. There was no point in being around him, even though she wanted to see him. Which was why she couldn't. Or wouldn't. No need to put herself into a situation where she might accidentally bump into him, when it was just as easy to avoid him altogether.

On a ship this large, after all, avoidance was fairly simple. Which was her reason for being there in the first place—to make her life simple by taking a detour around everything that adversely affected her.

So now here she was, all alone on the promenade deck, going for a stroll on a perfectly beautiful evening. Being alone wasn't such a bad thing, really, even though the people around her did make her uneasy, all those couples on romantic interludes, walking hand in hand, stealing the occasional kiss, embracing in hidden alcoves, doing what couples should be doing on a night such as this. The sounds of happiness off in the distance added to the ambiance— lively music filling the empty spaces, laughter bubbling through the air, both coming from the people enjoying themselves at the formal dance being held in the grand ballroom this evening.

She'd received an invitation to attend, with a little note tucked inside telling her that the ship had a limited number of escorts available for those who were alone on the cruise. In her fantasy, the invitation was from Michael, but in reality the stamped scrawl on it was a fuzzy blue duplicate of the captain's signature, probably put there by one of the ship's office staff and never even seen by the captain himself. "For the best," she murmured.

Sarah strolled casually along the railing, looking out into the water at the reflection of the ship's twinkling lights dancing off the gentle waves made by the ship as it glided along its way rather than watching other people doing the things she was, surprisingly, envious about. She should have flown back home. That chance came up earlier today, yet she hadn't even so much as flinched when the announcement had been made. Now she was wondering why she'd stayed here, given her troubling proximity to Michael. Perhaps it was that she had to be somewhere, and on board a cruise ship was as good a place as any.

Or maybe it was because of Michael? Something to do with her growing attraction?

No, that wasn't it. Absolutely, positively, could not be! He was handsome. Had a nice personality. He was an outstanding doctor. *Wonderful, amazing kisser.* But all those things combined weren't enough to sway her over to the side she so arduously resisted—the side where she found herself solidly involved with someone again. Been there, done that, twice now, and she couldn't go back. Sure, she was an emotional wreck over the choice she'd made to stay unattached in every way, because she loved being involved. Loved everything about it. But once with Kerry, then a second time with Cameron...

Sarah truly didn't believe in the third time being the charm, which was why she was a mess now because, deep down, she really did want to give that third time a chance. But being a mess was easier because the only pain was self-inflicted, which was much easier to endure than what she already had.

"Did you know you've become quite famous?" A bright, chirpy voice from behind her interrupted her thought. "People are talking about what a brave thing you did to help that little boy, the way you put your life on the line to save him."

Sarah spun around to face her admirer, not because she wanted any kind of a conversation with the woman but because she wanted to be polite. "I wasn't really brave. I think I just did what anybody would have done under the circumstances." What her natural instincts had led her to do.

"Well, from what I've heard, there weren't a lot of people stepping up to help, Sarah. And you were the one who went under that bus and stayed there when they had to move it off him. I'd say that's risking your life."

The woman looked vaguely familiar, but Sarah couldn't

quite place her. "Do I know you?" she asked. "Have we met before?"

"We haven't been properly introduced, but I suppose you could say we met that day in the elevator, when you nearly fainted in my arms and Dr Sloan caught you. My name is Martha. Martha Grimes."

Now she remembered. The lady with the big, purple hat.

"I heard mention that you were a doctor," Martha continued. "That explains why you did what you did for that child. Even though you're trying to be modest about it, it's in you to be brave like that, to help somebody in distress. I know how it is. My husband was a doctor and he'd have done the very same thing you did."

"A doctor," Sarah murmured, still trying to be polite to Martha yet not really in the mood for conversation.

"A very good doctor. Gone a year now. It was so sudden. He hadn't been sick a day in his life, then all of a sudden…"

Martha's voice was positively sad, and in the light shining down on them from one of the lanterns hung along the walkway Sarah could see the woman's eyes pooling with tears. Her heart went out to Martha because she, too, knew the pain of loss in the same deep, personal way.

"What kind of doctor was he?" Sarah asked gently.

"Obstetrician." Martha's voice was filled with pride as she fought back the sniffles. "I was his office nurse, helped him deliver babies until I started having babies of my own." She swiped at a stray tear trickling down her cheek. "Now here I am, on a cruise my husband and I should have been taking together, only I'm with the Ladies' Purple Hat League. We do gardening in public areas to make things beautiful. Planting purple flowers…" She started getting tearful again, and fumbled through her purse for a tissue. "Purple pansies and petunias our specialty."

"Purple flowers, like your purple hats," Sarah said sympathetically.

Martha laughed. "You can't miss us, can you? We do tend to stick out wherever we go." She was still dabbing at tears, sniffling again and biting her bottom lip to keep from crying harder. "You'll have to forgive me. I'm new at this…at being alone. It's not easy being all by myself after forty years of marriage."

Yes, that was something Sarah understood all too well. Married to Kerry only a little over a year, she'd wept for months after he'd died. She couldn't even imagine what it would be like to lose the person you loved after forty years with him. Poor Martha. Yet she was getting on with her life through her Purple Hat League, which was more than Sarah could say for herself. It was commendable, not that *she'd* ever don a purple hat herself, but she did admire Martha for what she was doing, fighting her way through while her heart was still breaking. "Look, would you care for a ginger ale? I know this nice little lounge…"

Before she could finish, Martha pulled Sarah into her ample bosom and practically squeezed the breath out of her. Ten minutes after that and they were tucked away in Sarah's favorite booth, sipping ginger ale and chatting like old friends. Well, one old friend and one woman who wasn't saying so much. But Sarah didn't have to say much around Martha, and Martha didn't seem to notice. Even so, she truly could have done a lot worse for a companion. Martha Grimes was a pleasant, if not overly talkative woman, and she actually seemed to enjoy the karaoke singer, who was doing a particularly agreeable job.

Twenty minutes of ginger ale, chat and karaoke had passed before Sarah saw Michael approaching her. Maybe it was a good thing she had Martha here with her tonight, because he looked especially attractive in a well-worn, faded pair of blue jeans that hugged him in all the right places and a cream-colored cableknit sweater that accented everything she liked accented in a man. "Michael," she said, giving him a cordial nod, even though her pulse was racing when he stepped up to the table.

"Sarah," he said, just as cordially. He glanced at Martha, turning on a much broader smile for the older woman.

Sarah made the proper introductions, explained that Martha was one of the ladies in purple hats, then let Martha launch into her explanation of why they wore purple hats and what kinds of flower varieties they planted, while Sarah sat back and observed Michael…her observations first coming as a woman but then as a doctor when she noticed that he seemed particularly tired tonight, and that his limp was far more pronounced than before. The doctor in her took over completely as he stood there awkwardly, listening to Martha ramble on and on. It wouldn't be proper to ask him how he was feeling, even though she was tempted, because that could signal involvement and that was the last thing she wanted, especially after what had happened two nights ago. But he was a doctor, too. If he needed help, wouldn't he get it?

Silly question. Doctors were the worst when it came to getting help for themselves. Cameron came to mind in that category. He had been an excellent doctor, her medical partner actually, and someone whose skills and decisions she'd trusted implicitly. Yet when his symptoms had started, he'd written them off as fatigue. Fatigue! Weeks and weeks later, it had been discovered he'd had a well-progressed case of leukemia. That was the one single experience that had taught her how the worst patient of all was a medical doctor. Especially a doctor diagnosing himself the way Cameron had done. So it was only normal that she didn't have much of an expectation of Michael paying attention to what was going on with himself. Yet it wasn't her place to get involved, even if she was bothered by the way he favored his right leg, shifting his weight off it then back onto it, and wincing slightly as he did so.

"Michael, I, um…" she started, but was interrupted by

Martha scooting her way out of the booth. The karaoke machine had just become available and Martha was on her way to have a try at a Beatles classic. As she breezed by Michael, he finally sat down next to Sarah. "She seems nice enough," he said in a lackluster voice, keeping quite a distance from her.

"She's lonely. Widowed only a few months, and she doesn't know what to do with herself. I don't think planting purple flowers is very fulfilling for her."

"It's nice that you've befriended her."

His voice was so stiff it was almost unrecognizable. After convincing herself that what had happened at Evangeline's was nothing to be embarrassed by, was it possible that Michael was embarrassed? "Not befriended so much as I do sympathize with her. My husband died a few years ago, and I know how it feels to be so…alone. Not knowing where you're going or what you're going to do. It's frightening. You spend half your time hoping no one will notice you and half your time praying they will."

Michael looked shocked by Sarah's admission…properly shocked. "I didn't know, Sarah! I'm…I'm sorry."

"I appreciate it. But you couldn't have known because it's nothing I bring up in the course of normal conversation. You know, *Hello, my name is Sarah Collins, and I'm a widow.* It makes people uncomfortable. They don't know what to do or say around you, and they feel embarrassed or awkward because they're unsure about what's proper under the circumstances, so it's best left private, I think." It was something a man who'd had his tongue down her throat should know, however.

"How long were you married, if you don't mind me asking?"

"Just over a year."

He nodded, the way people usually did when they heard the story. However, most of them prodded her for more information about Kerry's death, asked tacky questions, made insensitive comments like *Well, thankfully you'd only been married a year. It would be so much harder on you if you'd been married longer.*

"I know words really are never enough, but I *am* sorry, Sarah," he said again, at the same time Martha hit an operatic note in a range the Beatles had never achieved and people in the lounge spontaneously jumped to their feet, applauding her. "I do have some idea what it's like going through what you did, and I know it's not easy, no matter how long you were married. Losing someone you care about…someone you love—is hard. Cruel. It hurts on so many levels, and I'm sorry you've had to go through that."

"Thank you. It was quite a while ago, but I do know how difficult it is to get over it, which is why I thought Martha needed a friend tonight. She's not doing so well yet, and she shouldn't have to be by herself."

"Your husband. Was he a doctor?"

Sarah shook her head. "An engineer. He built bridges. Had quite a good reputation for it, actually. In fact, I met Kerry on a bridge. I was strolling, totally absorbed by the sights of the river down below, and he was strolling, looking at ways to overhaul the bridge, totally absorbed by the support structures. He literally bumped into me—the movable romantic force meets the immovable scientific one, we always said. I discovered his melanoma…on our honeymoon.

"Was it metastatic?" Cancer that had spread.

She nodded, amazed by how easy this was. What was it about Michael that made this so easy when telling other people had always been so difficult? "Stage four." Meaning severe. "It wasn't diagnosed in time, unfortunately. We did everything possible, he had every treatment. But the different things we tried couldn't keep up with it. In the end, the cancer spread to his bones, then to his lungs within a matter of a few months. Kerry's oncologist thought it had probably been there a while, but by the time I discovered it, it was already too late."

"They do go unnoticed much of the time," Michael said, taking hold of her hand and giving it a squeeze.

"Yes, they do," she said simply. That much was true, but a fiancée should have noticed it some time during their six-month relationship and subsequent two-month engagement. It had been a tiny speck just under his armpit—but she hadn't seen it. New love, with all its excitement and urgency, didn't really have much to do with physical exams, and with so many other wonderful places and sensations to explore, she'd just never looked there. Not until their wedding night, after they'd made love for the first time as husband and wife. Totally satiated, Kerry had lain back on his pillow, his hands cupped behind his head, grinning at her with all the contentment in the world, and she'd seen it. There were no words to describe what she'd felt at that moment. How could there be words to describe what, as a doctor, the newly wed wife had known she'd found? "Well, it looks like our diva has left the stage," she said, deliberately changing the subject as Martha headed back to the table, taking a bow every few steps of the way as the people in the lounge continued to applauded her.

Michael took that as a hint, and pulled away from Sarah.

"You don't have to go," Sarah said, disappointed that he was. He was easy to talk to. Easier than anyone she'd ever known in her life, and that included the two men she'd loved.

"I'm afraid I do. It's been a long day. Two of my medics are sick and I only stopped here to grab a sandwich to take back to my cabin. I've got to be back on duty in four hours and I need to get some sleep. Any other time…" As he stood, he brushed his thumb over her cheek. "Any other time, Sarah," he said on a wistful sigh, then turned away.

"Can I help you?" she cried out impulsively as the karaoke revved back up with a duo intent on butchering a ballad. "Can I help you in the hospital?" Volunteering for medical duty hadn't been her intention, but she was worried about Michael. He needed more than four hours of sleep, and his limp as he left the table was even more pronounced than his limp toward the table had been a few minutes earlier. "I can do, well, whatever you need me to. Lab work, general checks, anything. I'm not busy, and I could…"

He turned back to face her. "I appreciate that, but we're fine so far. We still have adequate coverage with the staff we have, even if we're putting in longer hours."

"Longer hours, and you're not looking good, Michael." There, she'd said it, even though she hadn't meant to. But it had just popped out. "You look…tired."

He opened his mouth to say something, then changed his mind as Heidi, the waitress, wiggled her way up to him and handed him a white paper bag with his sandwich in it. He thanked her, said goodnight to Martha, who'd climbed back into the booth, then he took a long, hard look at Sarah, but said nothing. All he did was smile, then walk away.

"Nice-looking man," Martha commented. "Downright handsome. You two are friends? Maybe even something more? A shipboard romance, perhaps?"

"We met that day in the elevator, when I collapsed in his arms. That's the extent of our relationship," she lied, even though they'd met in some fashion, personal or impersonal, almost every day since then. Was that enough to call him a friend? Was their volatile chemistry enough to call it something more? The fact that she rarely revealed that she was a widow to anybody, including Martha, and it had been so easy talking about it to Michael probably did make him a friend. She'd admit to that much and draw the line there, because one step over it put her back at Evangeline's, and that was something she really didn't care to explore further.

So, for the duration of the cruise, Michael Sloan was her friend. That was a decision with which she was satisfied.

But what would happen after the cruise?

Would he go off to his world and she back to hers?

Somehow that seemed inevitable, yet Sarah caught herself wondering if it would seem strange to book herself on the next cruise after this one, just to spend a little more time with Michael. "He's a nice man," she agreed on a melancholy note. The starkest truth of her world was that she might yearn, but she would never touch again.

"You two look so good together," Martha said. "The way my Robert and I did when we were younger."

Maybe that was true, but she'd looked good with Kerry, too. People had commented on that, especially on their wedding day. And she'd looked good with Cameron, something that had been said over and over at their engagement party. How did that old saying go? Was it, once bitten, twice shy? Could she change that to twice bitten and third time scared to death?

The truth was, she was attracted to Michael in ways she'd never meant to be attracted again. She would like to look good with him. No, she would *love* to look good with him, a sentiment that was speeding up her pulse rate and turning her respirations rapid and shallow. *That was the problem.* "You know what, Martha? You have a lovely voice. After these two guys get off the karaoke, I'd love to hear you sing again."

He'd worked harder than this, but he couldn't remember a time when he'd worked in a more distracted condition than he was right now. Sarah was on his mind all the time. After going for so long without any emotional involvements, finally convincing himself that he could get along fine without one, here he was, thinking about something that just couldn't happen. Not now. Especially not with someone who'd already known more than her fair share of tragedy. How could it be fair to her, dragging her into his own tragedies?

Knowing that he had to put an end to this kind of wasteful thinking, however, wasn't stopping him from imagining all the things he wouldn't allow himself to have. And as his patient load was growing, and as he wandered from patient to patient, treating all the common shipboard maladies overtaking passengers, he couldn't help but wonder how it might have been to work alongside her. She'd volunteered, after all. So he could have said yes, could have taken her up on her offer then scheduled her to work when he worked, saying, of course, that he was duty bound to keep a close eye on her as she wasn't a regular ship's employee.

Duty bound! Just like he'd been duty bound to seduce her in Evangeline's hallway then, later on in the booth, kiss her like he'd never kissed another woman. After all that, there wasn't an excuse on the face of the earth that he could use to keep Sarah at his side—not one she'd believe, anyway. Especially when the only thing he really wanted to do was finish what they'd started that night. Wanted it so badly he wasn't even sure he could work alongside her and remain unaffected.

Except there was one big thing standing in the way of letting her work with him, as much as he'd wanted to accept her suggestion…one big thing that set him right back into the professional frame of mind. Sarah had never confided her reason for not practicing medicine now, and that was a huge concern. While he couldn't imagine Sarah ever doing anything wrong as a doctor, anything that would have had devastating results or even have gotten her sanctioned in some way, he did have to know about her background and her reason. That was ship's policy, and he had to be careful with the way he proceeded as the responsibility of the ship's hospital was solely his. But more than that, as a responsible physician, it was his own personal policy to know about the people who treated his patients. So, with the remote possibility that she could have had her medical license revoked, which he doubted, he couldn't allow her to work. As much as he would have liked to. *Loved to!*

"We've had thirteen new people come in with generalized aches, low-grade fever, lung congestion in the past three hours," Ina, the nurse in charge, reported to him. "Most of them can stay in their cabins and no one feels all that bad. Oh, and we're having the normal lot of over-eaters, people who are seasick, pulled muscles, that sort of thing. Nothing you wouldn't expect to see."

Michael sighed, looking at the growing stack of patient charts on his desk. That was the part he truly hated—the paperwork. "Well, you can't do much about the people with the flu-like symptoms, but you'd think some of the others would apply common sense with their eating habits, wouldn't you? I mean, the stomach's only got so much elasticity to it, and it gets to a point where it won't stretch any more. And then their food choices…" He faked a shudder. "Like I said, no common sense at all."

"Like you have when you eat those huge, porky, greasy Cubanos every day?"

"And what's your point?" he asked, chuckling.

"Other than the fact that you have horrible dietary habits yourself, and that you're in a rut with what you eat? Probably nothing, unless you want me to say something about the way you've look lately, because that's not too good. Or the way you've been limping, because that's not too good, either. Or the overall rut your whole life is in, which isn't healthy for you, Mike. You're too young to be acting like an old man. Which is what you're doing."

"I already have a mother, Ina," he said, trying to sound good-natured, even though he was a little put off by her observations. He'd have been even more put off if they weren't true. But they were, and he knew it. He was in a rut in so many ways, and it was easy to get lazy like that. Easier than trying to crawl out of that rut. It was all taking its toll on him, too, both physically and emotionally. Especially these past few days.

"And your mother's not here, seeing what I'm seeing. So, until she is…"

He thrust out his hand to stop her. "I'll eat better and sleep better. Is that good enough?"

"I won't tell you how to run your personal life, but at least have someone look at your leg. Because you need that, too."

Touchy subject. He didn't really talk about it unless someone like Ina forced him to. "My leg is fine," he snapped. It did tend to bother him the more tired he was. His emotional turmoil was beginning to drag him down physically. But there was an easy cure for that and maybe he'd take a week off after this cruise was over, just to rest. It was all part of the same restlessness.

"No, it's not, or you wouldn't be so grumpy about it."

"If you weren't such a damned good nurse, I'd fire you," he grumbled.

"If I weren't such a damned good nurse, I wouldn't care what's going on with you. But I am, and I do, and you know I'm right, even if you won't admit it out loud. So, how about a cup of tea?"

Ina's hideous brew from hell. He really should tell her how bad it was, declare it a hazard of some sort, then take her teapot and throw it overboard. But he wouldn't be that unkind to someone who thought she was doing a good thing, even if that good thing turned his stomach. "I'd love a cup of tea," he said, fighting back a cringe.

An hour later, back in his cabin, he rinsed the aftertaste of Ina's tea from his mouth and turned on the shower to let the water warm up. Now that he was off duty again, he had eight blessed hours before he went back on duty, and he intended to spend each and every one of them with his eyes closed. Unless, of course, he got called back, which was a possibility with another of his medical crew taken ill in the past hour.

Pulling off his white uniform shirt, Michael dumped it into the laundry bag and was starting to unzip his pants when a knock on his door stopped him. His first thought was that he was already being called back and he hadn't even been off fifteen minutes yet. "I'm coming," he called, grabbing his shirt out of the laundry bag. He was shrugging it back on as he opened the door, expecting to see Ina standing there with another cup of tea. Instead, he saw Sarah.

"I don't want to bother you," she said, "but I wanted to talk about my offer. I heard someone else on your crew is sick." Her eyes raked over his chest. "And I…um…I wanted to tell you that I'm serious. If you need me to come and work…"

Two of the purple-hat ladies, obviously lost and wandering down a passage where they weren't supposed to be, took a look at Michael in his half-dressed condition, then started to titter. "Come in," he muttered, grabbing Sarah by the hand and pulling her into his cabin, then shutting the door behind him.

"I'd expected something bigger," she said, looking around the room. "Since you practically live here, I thought you'd have larger quarters than the passengers have."

He laughed. "They're large, if you're not claustrophobic and don't have a lot of personal possessions." Which he did, but they were in storage back in Florida. His real life all locked up safely while he lived this life.

"I meant what I said, Michael. I want to help in the hospital. Whatever you need me to do is fine."

Maybe he would take up her offer. With the right permissions, it could work out. Having a little more time with her wasn't a bad incentive either. "Can you give me ten minutes to shower, then we'll discuss it? I'd like to get myself cleaned up before we talk about anything, if you don't mind."

"Should I come back later? Or do you want to meet me somewhere else?"

"No. This if fine. Just make yourself comfortable here. Like I said, ten minutes."

Michael disappeared into the bathroom and Sarah could hear the water running. She sat in the single chair in his cabin, feeling awkward, three steps away from his bed, fighting back the fantasies assailing her. On top of that, the purple-hat ladies outside were probably spreading rumors that turned her fantasies into reality, but the truth was that, she really had come here to offer her services again. *That's all!* While she didn't want to return to work on a regular basis, the urge to get back into it for a little while was taking over, and getting back into it with Michael at her side certainly had more than its fair share of appeal.

But right now, as she waited, she was so close to his bed she could smell the slightly musky scent of his aftershave, probably permeating his sheets. Musky sheets. Then all of a sudden she was picturing his bare chest, and the way his partially zipped white uniform pants had ridden low on his hips, revealing the sexiest patch of dark hair trailing below his belly button.

All of a sudden she felt hot. Jittery. It wasn't a panic attack this time though. Not in the traditional sense, anyway, as the panic she was feeling had much more to do with a dormant libido waking up—waking up, screaming—than it did the walls closing in on her. Which they weren't doing, amazingly enough.

Walk, Sarah. Just walk it off.

But she didn't want to walk out of his cabin as the reason for her being there was, truly, to offer her help. It was genuine. She did want to help.

Shake it off before he comes back. Shake what off? The fact that she could picture herself between the sheets with him? That her cheeks were flushed? Or that her hands were shaking?

Or that she was merely giving in to all the silly romantic

notions of a cruise and this wasn't at all about Michael? That was probably the one she didn't want to shake off, the only thing in these past few days that made any sense to her.

Except knowing that and walking straight through his door, back into the corridor, back to her cabin, were things that didn't seem to mesh so well because here she was, still ignoring what was becoming increasingly obvious to her…almost as obvious as the steam that was seeping into the room from underneath the bathroom door.

She was getting hotter by the minute. Steam, yearning, raw emotions, both old and new, it all caused her to jump up from her chair and start pacing. Back and forth, round and round. The space was too small to take many steps, but she walked from one end of his bed to the other, back and forth to his closet, to the cabin door, forming a precise rhythm to her steps so she could count off the cadence rather than think about anything.

This is crazy, Sarah. OK, so a little thinking was sneaking in.

You're attracted to the man, so why not admit it? Especially after she'd crawled all over him already. But was this more than a physical attraction? That notion was slipping in, which scared her. Admitting to something physical was one thing, but to something more…

"Too much thinking," she muttered, deciding this wasn't a good idea. She still wanted to volunteer, but she couldn't stay in his cabin. The feelings and awareness were squeezing her out. She'd leave him a note, telling him she'd catch up with him later.

Good idea. Get out of his cabin before he was out of the shower because Michael in the shower was too potent an image for her to deal with.

In a hurry to leave, Sarah searched the nightstand next to his bed for a piece of paper and a pen, but no luck. The was nothing on the little table in the corner but a stack of medical textbooks. So she decided to check his closet, not to go through personal belongings or anything like that, but to see if what she needed was in there.

When she opened the door, her eyes went immediately to the array of white uniforms hanging in a neat row. *He looked so good in his uniform*. Then to the few off-duty clothes he had hanging there. *He looked good in those, too*. She didn't see a pen on the shelf, and when she glanced down she saw shoes, and a…

Dear God! It was a prosthetic leg.

Michael's limp!

How could she not have recognized it?

The way she hadn't noticed Kerry's melanoma or recognized Cameron's leukemia. That's how!

Taking two steps back, she bumped straight into Michael. She turned, stared him straight in the eyes, then drew in a sharp breath. "I changed my mind. I don't want to work for you."

After that, Sarah walked very calmly to Michael's door, turned the handle, then left the cabin. And slumped against the wall outside while her whole body began to tremble.

How could she have ever thought she could be a practicing physician again when she couldn't even see the things she should have, the things that were so close to her?

CHAPTER SEVEN

MICHAEL stared at the cabin door for a moment, then finally looked into his open closet. What he saw first…his running prosthesis, one made especially for the hard, pounding run he liked to have three times a week, four if he could fit it in. Was that what had caused Sarah's reaction? She'd seen it, been repulsed, then left?

Surely she'd known about it, hadn't she? He always limped a little, even on his best days, and Sarah did have a trained eye, so she must have noticed it. Then again, maybe she hadn't. And it wasn't like he'd slipped a mention of his injury into his casual conversations, because he never discussed it with anyone. Not even Ina. But he didn't keep his amputation a secret either. If someone asked a question it, he answered. Sarah, though…he'd really thought she would have known, would have seen it.

Or perhaps, deep down, he'd hoped she wouldn't.

He hadn't been involved with anyone as a casual friend, or even as a lover, since he'd been jilted after his injury. Emotionally, he wasn't ready for it yet—a fact of which he was painfully aware. Something else he was just as painfully aware of was what he had to do before he could ever hope to have a semblance of a normal life again. But that had much more to do with the circumstances surrounding his injury and not the injury itself. Sometimes, though, it all blurred together…the loss of his leg, the loss of his dream, the loss of himself all tied up in there somewhere.

Could, or would, he ever let himself fall in love again? Yes, he had thought about what could happen if he ever did, thought about what kind of woman would be attracted to someone like him, to someone disabled the way he was. He tried not to, though, because he wasn't at a place in his life where any of that would fit in.

Of course, he'd be lying to himself if he said it didn't bother him—not the injury itself as much as what might come about as a result of it. That wasn't the reason he'd avoided any number of women who'd made advances these past months since he'd come to work as a ship's doctor. Or the reason he'd avoided even looking at them. Heaven knew, he wasn't a saint when it came to that part of his life. Wasn't even close to it. He'd had relationships, long and short. He'd had his share of casual flings, short and shorter, too. Quite a vigorous, healthy past, all things considered. Yet right now getting involved in *any* manner wasn't right, not when he had so little to offer someone.

So little to offer himself, for that matter.

But Sarah…she was different. Someone who intrigued him. Someone who had captured his interest and held it. Someone so sexy and yet so vulnerable he couldn't even begin to imagine what it would be like to have a woman like that in his life for a little while, maybe even for ever. He hadn't meant to look, hadn't meant to go any further after he had. Just look at him, though, all caught up in thoughts he simply didn't need to be having. Sarah was on his mind in ways he didn't want, and couldn't control, and he was disappointed by her reaction to his prosthetic leg. More than disappointed, he was surprised.

Better to find out now, he supposed, unable to shake off the letdown seeping through him as he sat down on the edge of the bed, getting ready to sleep. What had he expected, though? It wasn't like this was the first time someone was turned off by him. It wouldn't be the last time either.

Sinking back into the pillows, Michael stared up at the ceiling for much longer than he cared to before he finally dozed off. But it was a fitful sleep that overtook him, not at all restful, and when he woke up seven hours later he felt agitated and restless—much worse than he had before he'd gone to sleep. Naturally, the first thing that came to his mind when he opened his eyes was Sarah.

"Damn," he muttered as he crawled out of bed. Here it was, another day, another dozen or so patients to see, and he just didn't have the energy for it. Didn't have the energy for any of it.

And that had nothing to do with the fact that in spite of everything, in spite of not knowing what he wanted to do with his future, he still loved being a doctor. Loved it, lived it, breathed it like it was the very oxygen he needed. No, his lack of energy for it today had nothing to do with the job itself but with all the uncertainties of it he'd yet to face. The time was coming, though. He could feel it in his bones. Or maybe it was the way he couldn't get Sarah off his mind that was causing the change in him. Perhaps seeing how adrift she was in her life made him realize just how adrift he was in his own.

Whatever the case, as he trudged off to work that morning he felt the changes coming.

"Morning, Mike," Ina said brightly as he walked through the hospital entry. She immediately handed him a cup of her special brew, the way she did every morning.

This morning, though, Michael didn't even muster a polite smile when he handed it back to her. "No more tea," he told her, rather gruffly.

"But I thought you liked my tea."

She sounded positively hurt. Hurt, like the way he still felt after Sarah's reaction last night. No reason he should feel that way and he couldn't explain why he did. But rather than think about it, or even deal with Ina and her repulsive tea, he simply took the mug back from her and continued walking on to his little office, where he had himself one good look at the growing stack of paperwork he needed to do and slumped down into his desk chair, really hating this day, even though it had barely begun. "Have Dr Monty see patients for the next hour while I try to get caught up with all this mess," he called out to Ina, who was organizing patient charts in the outer office. "And if he doesn't have anyone come into the clinic first thing this morning, tell him to go ahead and do rounds in the hospital."

"Doctor Monty is sick this morning. Flu symptoms. He called in about fifteen minutes ago and said he won't be back for at least twenty-four hours. Twenty-four, if he's lucky."

Michael let out an exasperated sigh. "Another one?" This was beginning to worry him because it had all the makings of some kind of virus spreading through his crew. And as the crew succumbed so went the passengers. "Dr Griswold? I know he just went off duty, but I need him back on, at least for the next hour."

"You're right. He just went off duty, but he's not feeling too well either, and I have an idea he's already in bed." Ina stepped into Michael's office. "I didn't want to be the bearer of bad news, but we're down by well over half our staff now. You're the only doctor out of four who's not sick, and besides me there are only two other nurses left. And if you want my opinion, I think we could be working up to an outbreak of norovirus." A highly contagious virus resulting in gastrointestinal upset and other associated belly symptoms, that usually lasted between twenty-four and sixty hours. Norovirus was notorious for spreading quickly on cruise ships because everyone lived at relatively close quarters, and while it wasn't an illness with a serious outcome, it was one that turned into a huge inconvenience for the passengers and an even bigger headache for the medical staff.

"Normal symptoms?" he asked. "I'm assuming it's running its normal course."

"Not yet. Most of the complaints so far are achiness, feeling tired, that sort of thing. But you know what happens next!"

He did. Hundreds of sick people, all confined to their cabins, all of them feeling like they were going to die even though they wouldn't, all of them wanting a doctor's attention, even when they didn't really need it. He'd heard about norovirus hitting ships—hitting them hard and knocking down hundreds—but this would be his first time, if norovirus was, indeed, what this was, and he wasn't looking forward to it. It wreaked havoc on a ship's medical facilities, not to mention its medical crew, which was already turning out to be the case, it seemed. "But *you're* feeling OK?" he asked Ina, trying to sound light about it, even though he was getting worried that she could be correct about her diagnosis.

"Maybe that's the question I should be asking you. Are you feeling OK? Because with the way you look this morning, not to mention the fact that you're grumpier than I've ever seen you…"

"I'm fine," he said, his voice completely flat. "Just dandy." Michael took a sip of his tea and maybe it was because he was getting used to it, or maybe she'd varied her usual atrocious recipe, but it didn't taste so bad to him. Was that a symptom of the virus he feared they were being infected with? Perhaps the first thing to go was the sense of taste.

"Well, from what I'm seeing, you're *not* fine, so is that because you don't feel well and you don't want to admit it, or is it personal? Something to do with that lady doctor you've been sniffing around after?"

"I'm not sniffing after the lady doctor," he snapped. "Or anybody else."

"You're not?" She snorted a laugh. "Just listen to you! I've never seen you act this way, Mike, and I've known you since you were a medical student." She'd worked at the hospital where he'd served his residency, and had proved herself the best nurse he'd ever seen. Opinionated, bossy, but the kind of nurse he wanted at his side, which was why he'd hired her out of retirement when he'd taken this job. "If I didn't know better, I'd say…"

He gave her a deep scowl, meaning to stop her. "*D*on*'t* say," he cracked. "Don't say a word. Not *one* word!"

"Grumpy *and* touchy," she persisted anyway. "I think she's really got you bothered, doesn't she?"

"Wouldn't matter if she does. She has a problem with…" He gestured to his right leg.

"You already got naked with her?" Ina asked, sounding almost excited about it. "It's about time you get back into life, act the way a normal man is supposed to."

"No, I didn't get naked with her, not that it's any of your business. But she discovered my running prosthesis in the closet, and that's as far as it went. She took one look and she was out the door."

"And you hadn't told her about your injury? Aren't you the one who tells the children at the amputee clinic to be honest about it?" He volunteered at a clinic in Florida when he had the chance…a few hours here and there. It had become something he looked forward to more than just about anything else in his life.

"Honest, yes. But I've never told them to just blurt it out without provocation. It's not exactly easy to drop the topic of amputation into casual conversation, you know, *Hello, my name is Mike Sloan and I have a right below-the-knee amputation.* Yeah, that's really going to impress someone."

"The *right* someone won't care." Ina shook her head and folded her arms across her chest. "But you're looking for any reason you can find not to get involved, and you sabotage your relationships, Mike. People do care. Old friends, new friends…people who wanted to be there for you after you were injured. You've shot them all down, and even now, if you meet someone and it looks to be a promising situation, you do something to kill it. And don't deny that, because you know you do. It's on purpose, and I'm not only talking about with the ladies. You push everybody away, and if I didn't just love you to pieces in spite of your attitude, you'd have pushed me away a long time ago, too."

Maybe what Ina said was true, all of it, but he wasn't going to admit it. "I don't have time for relationships."

"Because you don't want to make the time. But I've seen the way you look at Sarah, and it's a look I haven't seen in you before. Not back when you were a medical student, not since then either. Honestly, I've wondered if you might be falling in love with her, and now I know."

"Know what?" Michael snapped.

"That you're falling in love." She was so sure of it she almost seemed cocky. "Or you've already fallen in love. Too stubborn to admit it to yourself, though. And now you think you've got a reason to back away from it, just because of the way she reacted when she saw your prosthesis. You're probably glad of the excuse, aren't you? Glad Sarah gave you a reason not to have to come up with something yourself."

"Since when have I given you permission to get involved in my personal life?" he grumbled. "It's none of your damned business, Ina."

Rather than being offended, Ina laughed. "Like I said, now I have my answer. So, what are you going to do about it?"

"What am I going to do about a woman who's repulsed by the fact that I'm missing part of my leg? I think that already answers the question, doesn't it? There's not a damned thing I can, or will, do." The hell of it was, his leg wasn't even the problem.

"Not a damned thing to do except sit around and be

grumpy. Which you're very good at, Mike. And getting better at all the time. I'm betting it's not your amputation that turned her off, though. She probably got a big dose of your attitude."

"I'm not grumpy," he practically yelled.

Ina smiled at him with all the love of a mother, and her voice turned gentle. "Falling in love's not always easy, is it? But if it's meant to be, you'll find a way to work it out. Don't give up on it yet, Mike, and most of all, don't give up on yourself. You're quite a catch if you'll allow it, and if I were twenty-five years younger, I'd be giving that Sarah a run for her money. *A serious run.*"

They weren't docking anywhere today, but her bags were packed and ready to go for tomorrow. Aruba. She'd leave the ship there, spend a little time then fly home and start all over again—the cycle of her life now. For her, the cruise had ended, and so had the delusion that she could go back into medicine. One little incident with the boy under the bus, and she'd fooled herself into believing that something had changed, that all her imperfections had vanished. But, as she'd soon discovered, nothing had changed. Nothing at all. She was still the same Sarah Collins who had a confounding way of not seeing the flagrantly obvious—a horribly dangerous trait in a doctor.

"You're looking distracted this morning," Martha said. They were having breakfast together at an outside buffet near the pool. It hadn't been Sarah's idea to do it, as she'd have preferred staying cooped up in her cabin all day, having her meals delivered to her there. But Martha had come knocking on her door bright and early, and Sarah simply hadn't had the heart to refuse the woman a few minutes of conversation and companionship over buttered toast, fresh fruit and juice.

"I'm…um…I'm thinking about leaving the ship tomorrow and flying home," Sarah said, almost reluctantly. The truth was, leaving was purely an intellectual decision. It was the only practical thing to do under the circumstances. In her heart she wanted to stay, though. Yet she never let her heart win. Not any more. "It's something I've been thinking about from the start, but now's the time, so I'll be leaving once we arrive in Aruba."

Martha's eyes widened. "You're not having a good time? Or is this about a personal matter?"

A little bit of both. Even though it was something she couldn't put into words. "The cruise is not what I expected. I think maybe I'm more the type who prefers to keep my feet flat on the ground." Along with her heart.

"We're only halfway through. It would be such a shame to give it all up now. But I think it has to be difficult being here alone, the way you are. At least I have my purple-hat group."

Sarah grabbed a piece of ripe pineapple and offered it to Martha, hoping that would distract her from what Sarah believed would be the inevitable offer to join the purple-hat bunch as a way to keep her from being alone. "For some people, being alone is difficult, but I don't mind it so much. It keeps my life simple," she said. "And over the years I've learned that staying simple works best for me. I'm sure it seems dull to some, but I don't mind dull, because there aren't any complications."

"But the complications of friendships, and especially of a serious relationship…that's what turns a dull life into something that sparkles." Martha reached across the table and gave Sarah a friendly pat on the hand. "Sparkling is nice, Sarah, but I don't think you believe you're entitled to sparkle, do you?" Before Sarah could answer, Martha continued, "Look, some of the ladies and I are going to take a photography class they're offering on the ship. You're welcome to join us but, in my opinion, you'd be smarter chasing down that good-looking Dr Sloan. He's much more interesting than a snapshot, and as you're not going to stay with us much

longer I think your time would be better spent with him."
With those words, a definite sparkle popped into Martha's
eyes.

"I don't get involved," Sarah said, without explanation.

"Life isn't much fun without involvements. Planting
purple flowers certainly isn't something I've ever aspired to,
but if I didn't have my purple flowers, and the other ladies
who plant them along with me, I don't know what I'd do.
After my husband died I didn't think I ever wanted to be
involved with anything, ever again. But just look at me now!"
She reached up and cocked her purple hat. "I had to make
myself get involved, had to force myself to put this ugly hat
on my head and take that first step out my door, and I haven't
regretted a minute of it since I did."

"I've been involved," Sarah said, "and it's not all it's
cracked up to be. For me, I think the regret would be taking
the first step out the door." She shrugged a gloomy feeling
washed down over her, and turned her attention to the fresh
papaya juice she'd been nursing for the past several minutes.
The truth was, being involved was everything. She just didn't
have the heart to try it again.

Sarah spent another ten minutes lingering over a breakfast she wasn't in the mood to eat, listening to Martha ramble
on and on about all the things she'd done with her purple-hat
friends, before she decided to head back to her cabin
and…and do what? Spend the day sleeping, or staring at the
walls? Those were probably her best options, even though
they didn't seem much of a way to spend her last day at seas.
The thing was, what came next in her life? She'd leave the
ship, spend a few days in Aruba, then what was she going to
do after that? Take another trip? Was there really anything
left that she truly wanted to see?

The answer to that question was so obvious, she didn't
bother mulling it over in her mind. She didn't want to go
anywhere, didn't want to see anything, didn't want to do

anything. It was all as plain as that. Her life had become stagnant, and she hadn't even realized how much so until that day she'd crawled underneath the bus. Then it was like the floodgates had opened, and for one brief moment, she'd thought she could get back everything she'd always wanted. She wanted to work as a doctor again. Wanted it so badly it was turning into a physical ache. Wanted to diagnose and treat patients, again, wanted to be part of the whole medical community the way she had once been.

But the medical community deserved better than what she could give them, and that was always the bottom line that came back to flog her. She couldn't have what she wanted. Couldn't even come close to it.

When breakfast was over, Martha trotted off to her purple-hat ladies and Sarah headed back to her cabin. On the way she stopped and leaned against the ship's rail, simply to stare out at the ocean. It was one vast surface with so little on the top of it and so much underneath, all of it coming from nowhere, going nowhere. Like her.

"It's amazing, isn't it?" Michael said, stepping up beside her. "The first time I ever saw the ocean I was five years old. I went to the beach with my parents, and I think I spent most of the day trying to see the other side of the world. I knew it had to be out there somewhere, if only I could look a little harder. Once I was sure I spotted the other side of it, then it turned out to be a freighter making its way slowly across what I knew had to be the very edge of the world. I couldn't take my eyes off it, and I ran along the beach as it started to disappear, trying to keep it in my sight. I just knew that if I lost sight of it, it would fall off."

"But it didn't," she said, her voice wistful as she continued her stare, now visualizing a five-year-old spending his day doing the very same thing.

"No, it didn't. But I used up my whole day worrying about the people on that ship, worrying about what was out there at the end of the world. I could have been playing in the water with my brothers or building sandcastles or picking up sea-shells, but instead of doing the things a child should have been doing I found myself a little ridge and just sat there and watched. Wasted a perfectly good day doing nothing, as it turned out."

"Was it really a waste?" she asked.

He chuckled. "Actually, that was the day I announced to my parents that I wanted to be a doctor. Just like my father was, and my grandfather. In my five-year-old mind, I thought I could help all those people who were about to topple off the end of the world. Put bandages on them and make them better after their fall."

The way he made her feel better as she was toppling. "Then I'd say you were a little boy with strong convictions. When I was five I wanted to be a ballerina. When I was six I wanted to be a teacher. Then at seven an archaeologist. It was a pretty long list by the time I got to college, which was when I finally had to give it some serious thought and decide what I really wanted to do. But I'm sorry to say I didn't enter medical school with the conviction of a five-year-old boy who wanted to save a ship's crew from a terrible fate. I simply liked the science involved in medicine. Thought it was amazing. Thought the workings of the human body were the most interesting thing I'd ever encountered in my life." She turned to face him. "Look, Michael, I wasn't running away from your prosthetic leg," she said. "I know it probably looked that way to you, but that wasn't it, and I'm sorry I left you thinking so."

"It wouldn't matter if you were," he said, without a trace of defensiveness in his voice. "People react how they react. I've learned to deal with it."

"Or avoid it?"

"Has anybody ever told you how blunt you are?" he said, a hint of amusement in his voice.

She laughed. "It's been mentioned a time or two." She was dying to ask him about his injury, but so far he didn't seem willing to talk about it, other than in the vaguest sense. He'd said what he'd wanted to say, and that's all there was. "Blunt, stubborn…one of the technicians who worked for us at the clinic called me Dr Ice. She didn't know that I was aware of the nickname, but I wasn't bothered by it. It took me a long time to learn how to appear unaffected and, apparently, I was pretty good at it."

"Nothing about you seems unaffected to me. In fact, if your technician had seen you go under that bus with Delroy, and stay there the way you did, she'd find something else to call you. He's doing better, by the way. Good progress, according to his doctor."

Behind them, the frantic pounding of feet on the deck caught her attention for a moment, as one of the organized exercise groups fast-walked their way around the deck, their heel-toe, heel-toe rhythm almost precise as they passed by where Sarah and Michael were standing. As their footsteps faded she thought about how much she liked being here with Michael this way, and how she didn't want to leave. Which was exactly why she had to. Anything else got her involved, and she was so on the brink of doing just that she felt like the ship that five-year-old Michael Sloan had watched sailing along the edge of the world, ready to fall off. She was attracted to Michael Sloan, and it was about so much more than his ability to fill her medical longings. From that very first moment he'd caught her… No musings. No regrets. She plainly couldn't do this. "Look, Michael, about my offer to help you… I'm leaving tomorrow instead. I've already sent a message to the ship's captain telling him that when I go ashore in Aruba I won't be returning."

"Why?" His voice was stiff. That relaxed feeling between them was gone.

Should she tell him that she had feelings for him in a way

she didn't want to? Or tell him the same thing she told everybody else—that it was time to move on? That was always the easiest excuse. Very impersonal and precise, and no one could argue against it. But with Michael she didn't want to be impersonal and precise. She didn't see any other way, though. "My life is full of reasons, Michael. None of them really make any difference. I just do what I do, and moving on is part of that."

"Avoidance?" he snapped.

"Now aren't you the one who's being blunt?" Sarah smiled sadly, thinking about how true that was. But it was about self-preservation. She understood that better than she understood just about anything else. If you didn't avoid things, you opened yourself up to the possibility of being hurt, and she'd already had too much pain in her life.

He chuckled, but there was a sharp edge to it. "I've been called stubborn a time or two also."

"But never unaffected. The little boy who wanted to save that ship could never be unaffected. Neither could the man he turned into."

"Look, Sarah, if I weren't in trouble, I wouldn't say this, but I am. Most of my medical staff is down sick, and I need you to stay here and help me until the cruise line makes other medical arrangements. I've cleared you working here under emergency provisions through the ship's captain, who cleared it with the cruise line. So, until help arrives I'm authorized to do what I have to do to take care of the passengers and crew and for starters that's putting you to work. But I've got to warn you up front that we're looking at some hard hours ahead. There's a possibility we might have an outbreak of norovirus on our hands."

Sarah certainly knew what that was. Back in Boston, at her immediate care clinic, she'd treated a rash of people with norovirus, all of whom had jumped a quarantined ship that had been docked a few blocks from her office. "I take it you're confining them as they get sick?"

Michael nodded. "Both the passengers *and* my medical crew. If I had my way, I'd confine everybody on board, sick or not, for the next three days and let the whole damned thing run its course. Which they won't let me do. And to be honest, if this thing plays out the way it usually does, nobody's going to be allowed off the ship in Aruba anyway."

"Then I don't have much of a choice, do I?" The truth was, as much as she wanted to avoid practicing medicine, this unexpected opportunity excited her. Norovirus was simple. And she would have a little more time with Michael. That was, perhaps, the real reason she accepted. Around him she didn't feel quite so unaffected. In fact, if she wasn't very careful, he had the power to affect her in ways she'd thought she'd never be affected again. Only if she let that happen, of course. Which she wouldn't. "When do we start?" she asked, the gloomy shroud that had entangled her suddenly blowing out to sea.

CHAPTER EIGHT

"THREE passengers, all with non-specific complaints," Ina announced as Sarah followed Michael through the hospital doors. "Headaches, muscle aches, fever with unknown origin, several of them with some respiratory distress. That kind of thing. I've got them all in exam rooms, having their vitals taken and their medical histories assessed." Her glance darted from Michael to Sarah then back to Michael, and a thin little grin spread over her lips, even though she didn't break her cadence. "We've had calls from two more passengers who will be coming down here shortly, again non-specific complaints."

Sarah frowned. "Noro usually starts with quite a kick rather than non-specific complaints. This seems odd."

"But there are so many variations of it," Michael added. "Currently, there are five *known* specific norovirus groups that are divided into thirty-one smaller groups. The symptoms we usually see at the onset are generally the same, to varying degrees, but who knows? Viruses mutate so quickly these days we could be looking at a variant that hasn't been identified, or just a new version on an old theme."

"Well, identified or not," Ina chimed in, "the captain is on his way down to the hospital to see what we're dealing with. He says he wants a full report."

Michael nodded. It was premature to attach any major significance to this little rush of illnesses, but the captain should be made aware that there was a similarity, just in case it turned out to be something major. In the meantime, there were still the normal ailments to treat, and people were beginning to line up in the Emergency clinic to be seen. "Sarah, could you take over regular duty in emergency? I think that will be pretty much what you did working in an immediate care clinic. I'll back you up if you need it, look in on the patients already staying in the hospital, and I'll also take anyone coming in we think could be in the early stages of whatever this is. And, Ina…" He simply waved her off, as she was already on her way back to her nursing duties and needed no further instruction.

"Do I have a nurse?" Sarah asked.

"We're stretched pretty thin there, too. Besides Ina, we have two other nurses, and I'm going to try and keep them on general duty, triage, that kind of thing, if I can. If you need a nurse to assist you, call Ina and we'll see what we can do." He stepped closer, and took gentle hold of her arm. "You're going to do fine, Sarah," he said, his voice practically a whisper. "I know this isn't what you want to do, but I appreciate you helping me. It's safer having two doctors available." She looked worried, in spite of the fact that she was forcing herself to smile. But there was nothing else he could do at the moment.

Sure, it would have been nice working side by side with her, just to help boost her confidence a little. Or simply to spend a little time with her any way he could get it. That just wasn't going to happen today, though, and he wasn't worried about leaving Sarah on her own. She was a good doctor who, for whatever reason, didn't trust herself. That much was evident. He trusted her, though. And for now, that had to be enough. It would have been nice knowing what had caused the fear and doubt in her, but that was a story for another time. At present there were other priorities, and trusting Sarah was

one of them. She was good. He was sure of it—sure enough
to put the lives of his patients in her hands.

Her pace was slow at first, he noted. By the time she was
ready to start her medical duty, there were half a dozen
patients lined up waiting to be seen, and she took her time
seeing each one. He really didn't have time to stop and
observe, not that he would have, but he did catch occasional
glances of Sarah as she performed a routine procedure or
simply talked with a patient. What he saw was amazing. She
had such grace…something to which the patients were naturally drawn. He could see that in the easy smiles that came
over their faces once they were greeted by Sarah—the smiles
of a patient who truly trusted the doctor. It was nice, and he
would have loved standing back and watching, but Captain
Regard was waiting for him now, and it was time to have a
frank discussion about what was happening. In the past half-
hour another ten patients with the same non-specific complaints had wandered in. And in that same amount of time,
Dr Allen, one of the first people to go down with this
unknown ailment, had spiked an extreme fever and developed
a suspicious heart rhythm—so much so, they'd had to put him
on a monitor.

If this was norovirus, it was definitely an unknown strain,
as the formerly non-specific complaints were now becoming
specific, and they weren't anything like norovirus. That had
him concerned.

Captain Thomas Regard was a distinguished man. Tall, with
silver-gray hair and piercing blue eyes, he carried the
demeanor of ship's captain quite well, except that when
Michael set eyes on him, that demeanor was diminished.
Captain Regard looked gaunt, tired, and as he approached
Michael's desk, he practically fell into the chair opposite it.
"Report," he said, his voice weak. "Tell me what's going on
here. Why are most of your medical personnel down?"

"Symptoms?" Michael asked in return. "Tell me your symptoms."

Regard shook his head. "It's nothing. I'm due for some holiday time after this cruise, and once I've had a little rest I'll be fine."

"I have twenty people saying the same thing right now, Tom. And you're looking like every one of them"

"Is it norovirus?" the captain asked, his haggard face creasing into a frown. Noro was the scourge of so many cruise ships these days that it was well known to people, like Captain Thomas Regard, who had absolutely no medical knowledge whatsoever, except for Norovirus.

"Initially, that's what I thought. But now, I don't know. I'm inclined to think we've got something else going on…something in its very early stages. And based on what I'm seeing, the symptoms aren't even close to norovirus."

"So tell me what to do, Mike. You're the doctor here, and it's your call. Should we be alarmed?"

"Well, twenty's not an alarming number, if it doesn't go beyond that. But that's twenty people who've all come down with something I haven't been able to identify yet. I've got them confined to quarters but something's telling me that I need to bring them into the hospital to watch them even more closely. Especially if it's not norovirus, which is what I'm inclined to think right now."

Captain Regard nodded, although it was clear by the expression on his face that he didn't have the vaguest idea what Michael was talking about. "So, what about docking and going ashore in Aruba? Should we skip that port?"

"Yes," Michael said, without hesitation. "I don't know if we're dealing with something infectious, and I don't want to risk taking it ashore. So, at least for this port of call, we need to stay on ship."

"You know how that's going to go over, don't you, keeping the whole ship away from the next destination when only a handful of the passengers are sick? People aren't going to be happy." He let out a sigh. "And if I didn't feel like hell right now, I'd probably try and argue you out of this, but I do, so I won't." He started to stand, wobbled, and sank back down into the chair. Michael was immediately at his side, laying a hand on the captain's forehead at first, then taking hold of his wrist to feel his pulse.

"You're burning up with fever. And your heart rate is too fast. How long have you been sick?"

"About a day. But it'll pass," the captain said. "I'm going back to my quarters for a short nap now, and I'll be fine."

"You're off duty, Tom, and I'm admitting you to the hospital," Michael said emphatically, helping the man up from the chair.

"I need to—"

"There's nothing you need to do right now except rest and let me be the doctor." He expected an argument. The man had an exceptionally robust personality, but at this moment he had no fight left in him as he practically slumped against Michael, without uttering another word. Five minutes later, Captain Thomas Regard was the twenty-first patient on the charts for whatever this outbreak was. And there was no denying it. This was definitely an outbreak of some sort. As much as he hated admitting it, Michael was admitting it now.

"Your blood sugar is three times the normal value," Sarah said to the woman on the exam table. Mrs Margesson was the fifth over-indulger she'd seen that morning. Too much good food, too little willpower, and the result for a diabetic could be devastating. "Your blood sugar is registering at three hundred, and you need to be closer to one hundred."

The woman grinned sheepishly. "I ate a few sweets last night and had a pastry or two for breakfast this morning," she admitted. "I didn't think it would hurt me."

Sarah patted her patient's hand. "It's not much fun to

come on a cruise and not be able to eat everything they have available, is it?"

Mrs Margesson shook her head. "The food is so…good."

Wasn't this the same lecture Michael had given her, only in reverse? Eat more, Sarah. Don't let your blood sugar go so low. And hadn't she argued with him? Maybe this was some kind of retribution, being confronted with, well… herself. *Patience, Sarah*, she cautioned herself as she prepared to argue logic with a woman who was clearly more interested in a chocolate-covered éclair than she was a medical lecture.

"It's hard to resist," Gertie Margesson continued.

Sarah smiled, thinking back to the way Michael had handled her little blood-sugar situation. He really was an excellent doctor. She admired that in him. Wanted to emulate it right now. "Here's what I'd like to do, Gertie. First, I want to get your blood sugar back down to a normal level with some insulin. You're not so high that you're in any danger, but I really don't want you getting any higher because you do risk having a stroke in the short term, and I'm sure your own doctor has advised you of all the long-term side effects." Blindness, kidney failure, nerve damage, heart disease, circulatory problems leading to possible amputation…

Amputation! Was Michael a severe diabetic? That certainly was a consideration, and something she needed to watch him for since in the next little while he was going to be working more hours than he normally did. His blood sugar could go out of whack with extreme fatigue. "So, here's what you need to do after we've got your blood-sugar level back in order. I want you to watch your diet more closely, stay away from the sweets on a regular basis, restrict your carbohydrates overall. But just so you won't deprive yourself, I want you to go ahead and have a little indulgence every other day. Keep it moderate, though, and balance it out with a better choice of foods all the way around. In fact, I could have the ship's dietitian sit down and have a chat with you, maybe draw up your own special menu if you'd like. Also, you need to keep a record of your blood sugar. Test yourself three times a day and bring me the results every morning. If you're good, I'll give you the go-ahead for that little treat. If your results aren't so good, we'll hold off until they are. Can you do that?" She looked Mrs Margesson straight in the eye.

"That's asking an awful lot of me," Gertie replied, none too happy with any of this. She wanted more, but she needed less, and Sarah had a hunch that this wouldn't be the woman's last trip to the ship's hospital with a diabetic-related crisis.

"But you'll try," Sarah said.

"I'll try, but don't expect too much. I'm here on a holiday, and that includes my diet, so I'll be good when I get home."

Ah, yes. Put it off until tomorrow. She'd heard that excuse hundreds of times over the years. Deny the obvious now, promise to do better next time, and in the meantime hope the side-effects of what you're doing now don't do you in.

Wasn't that the way she was living, though? Didn't she put everything off until tomorrow, then the tomorrow after that? Didn't she keep promising herself that she'd make a decision about her life? Well, she understood Gertie Margesson's circumstances because, in a way, they were just like hers. Only Gertie did it with food, while she was doing it with avoidance. Yes, that old bugaboo she and Michael had already talked about. "I'm sure you do much better when you're home, Gertie, but if you don't do better here you might not make it home. Diabetes has serious consequences if you don't manage it properly. So, it's your choice. I can't control how you eat. Can't watch every bite you take. All I can do is try and fix you up if you hurt yourself, and hope it's enough."

Gertie looked like she'd been slapped in the face. Maybe it was a harsh pronouncement, but it was a true one. And for someone who had a history of missing the obvious, the way Sarah did, one thing she wasn't missing here was the fact that she had an uncooperative patient who truly believed that her actions today didn't have a significant bearing on her life tomorrow.

If only that were the case. But Sarah knew better, and all she had to do was remind herself of Kerry, and of Cameron.

After Gertie departed, not at all convinced by Sarah's little admonition to do better or else, there was no one left to see, so she wandered off in the direction of the clinic where Michael was working, ready to offer assistance. On her way, she glanced into one of the private patient rooms in time to see the man in the bed go completely rigid, then begin to thrash about so hard the bed rattled.

A seizure?

Sarah was immediately at his bedside, trying to turn him on his side in case he vomited up his stomach contents, but what she saw wasn't a seizure. The man was so cold his body was shaking as hard as a body could shake. And he was literally going stiff.

Rigor? "I need help in here!" she called, as the man frantically grabbed at her hand. His hand was icy. So were his cheeks, she found as she laid her hand on his face. His body was literally in the throes of what happened when someone froze to death, and it was hard to hear his heart beating as she pushed her stethoscope to his chest, he was thrashing and shaking so badly.

She listened for a moment, heard his heart beating rapidly, but not critically so.

"What do you need?" Ina asked, rushing in. She took one look at Captain Regard and ran right back out of the room.

"You're going to be fine," Sarah said, wrapping a blood-pressure cuff around the man's arm. "As soon as I make an assessment, we'll get you warmed right up." But what was making him so cold? That was the question she couldn't answer yet.

"What the hell?" Michael sputtered, running into the

room. "Fifteen minutes ago, when I admitted him, his temperature was spiking to four degrees above normal."

"And now it's dropped," Sarah said, stepping back as Ina shoved her way in to take Captain Regard's temperature. "To the point of rigors. What was your admitting diagnosis?" she whispered, pushing Michael out into the hall.

"Didn't have one. He's like the other twenty-five people we've admitted now, and I'm pretty damned sure it's not norovirus."

"Too bad," Sarah said. "With noro we know what to do." She breathed out an exasperated sigh. "Look, I know you're in charge here, but I think we need to set up an isolation ward until we can figure it out. Keep these people separated from everybody else, get the lab work started, treat the symptoms until we know what we're dealing with."

"His temperature's rising," Ina called out.

"Start an IV, normal saline for now. And get him on oxygen." Michael ran a frustrated hand through his hair. "And do the same for everybody else who's come in with the captain's symptoms."

"He's the captain?" Sarah asked.

Michael nodded. "Between us, I'm worried about how many of the crew are going to come down with this."

"What about medical supplies?"

"We're OK for now. Hope it stays that way until help arrives."

"Which will be when?"

He shrugged. "They're telling me soon, but not saying what that means. I have a suspicion the company is looking at its reputation, and sending in medical reinforcements to a ship with a couple of dozen patients with an undiagnosed illness is just bad publicity. They'll take care of us, but let's just say they'll be careful at first." He squeezed her arm. "I'm sorry I got you into this, Sarah."

"I'm not," she said, as one of the nurses ran by, carrying

an IV set-up. "Look, Michael. Can you spare me for a few minutes? I have an idea."

"Dr Sloan, the patient in number three is spiking a fever," the other nurse called from down the corridor. "And we have an ankle sprain in Emergency."

Before Michael could answer Sarah, she bolted out the door and ran straight to the elevator. Minutes later, she crashed through the doors to the photography class and ran toward the front of the room. Looking out over the group, she saw a sea of purple hats. "Martha," she called out, spotting her friend in the crowd. "I need your help. Now." Then she turned her attention to the rest of the ladies, who were whispering among themselves, wondering what was going on as the photography instructor assumed an angry frown over the intrusion. As Martha came forward, she whispered, "I don't have time to explain, and I don't want to cause a panic, but we need medical personnel in the hospital. *Now!*"

Martha acknowledged with a quick nod, then followed Sarah to the back of the room and waited until she had left before she looked around to see who in the class also had a medical background. Fifteen minutes later, after she'd discreetly called out four more purple hatters, the little troop of retired nurses marched their way into the ship's hospital, ready for duty.

"We're not going to put you in the ward where we're isolating the ones with the undiagnosed illness," she told Martha, who was wiggling her ample body into a pair of blue surgical scrubs. "We don't know what we're dealing with and I don't want to put any of you at risk, but what I'd like you to do is manage everything else that's coming in, which will allow Michael and me and the nurses already exposed to tend to the others." Which now numbered thirty-two.

"We don't need five nurses in the ER clinic," Martha stated. "So I'm coming with you."

"But we don't know what we're dealing with yet," Sarah argued.

"And if you get yourself too rundown, you won't be in any condition to find out. I know what I'm doing, Sarah. I spent my life working at a doctor's side, being in the thick of it, and that's what I do best."

Sarah gave the woman a big hug. "I think this is called getting involved," she said.

"In more ways than one." Martha chuckled. Backing away from Sarah, she grabbed an IV set-up from Ina, who was on her way into Dr Allen's room, and hurried to get to work.

"Where the hell did all those ladies out there come from?" Michael asked, minutes later, on his way back to the captain's bedside. Tom Regard's fever was on the rise again, and if the pattern repeated, he was about to drop to a nearly life-threatening cold shortly after.

"Purple hats, every last one of them. Desperate times call for desperate measures, and as you already had permission to find qualified help on board, that's exactly what I did."

"Well, I'll be damned," he said, as he swabbed the captain's arm, readying himself to take a blood sample. "We wouldn't happen to have a lab tech in the bunch, would we? Once I get the blood samples, I need someone to run them. My lab tech just checked herself into the hospital."

"Let me go and ask Martha."

Nine hours later, the crisis had not let up, and the slow trickle of patients into the emergency clinic continued. The cruise line was concerned now, and everything they needed was en route. Of course, with nine purple-hat nurses, two purple-hat lab technicians, and a retired purple-hat doctor who'd been called in by Martha and had subsequently taken total charge of all non-essential medical care, the hospital was functioning pretty well.

Captain Regard was doing better, after a simple prescription of acetaminophen, but he wasn't out of the woods. And unfortunately, Dr Allen had taken a critical turn. Michael hadn't left his side for the last hour as the man seemed to be suffering a serious cardiac crisis. Of the sixty-three patients they had in isolation now, seven were considered critical, nine were serious, and Dr Reese Allen, a man much too young and vital to be in his condition, was in a critical condition.

"Mike needs to take a break," Ina confided to Sarah. "He's not helping anybody, wearing himself out the way he is. But he won't listen to me."

"He's dedicated," Sarah said wearily. She'd been off her feet ten minutes, and was allowing herself twenty more, barring an emergency.

"Dedicated to the point of being foolish," Ina snorted. "Loosely translated to mean stubborn as hell."

"You've known him a long time, haven't you?" Sarah asked.

"I was the first face he saw the first time he stepped foot in a hospital. He was…different from the other medical students. They all huddled together, scared, timid, not sure which end of the thermometer to use. But Mike…he stepped right out, distinguished himself." She chuckled. "All full of big plans for his life."

"He was materialistic?"

"Not at all. Mike was about as altruistic as anybody I'd ever met. He always wanted to make a difference. Wanted to do something good with his life. Had so many goals, so many things he wanted to do as a doctor."

And he'd ended up here on a cruise ship? It wasn't a bad thing, and cruise ships did need medical personnel. But she seriously doubted that working on a cruise ship had been one of his goals, so what had happened to change him? His leg?

Sarah wondered about that, and she wanted to ask. She might have, but Ina dashed off in pursuit of an IV refill, leaving Sarah alone for the remainder of her break. At least, she'd thought she was going to be alone, but no sooner had Ina gone than Michael wandered into the doctors' lounge, and dropped his lanky body onto a sofa there, letting out a weary groan as he lifted his legs up over the armrest. "If I weren't so damned tired, I'd complain about how uncomfortable this sofa is," he said, as his eyes shut. "Oh, and *don't* let me sleep. I'm better off sleep-deprived than I am grabbing a quick nap."

"Medical school days," Sarah commented casually, giving him the full scrutiny of her medical expertise, studying him from head to toe while he wasn't looking. Such a handsome man. Better than handsome, actually. He was the kind of man who took away your breath at first glance. Rugged, even a little hard around the edges, he looked like a man who'd seen a lot of living. Of course, that was only conjecture, as she knew practically nothing about him. "Back then I was up for a quick nap anywhere, even standing up, if I had to."

He chuckled, but didn't open his eyes. "I remember once, I was so tired that I literally fell asleep sitting at a patient's bedside. When I woke up, a full hour later, I was still sitting in the chair, but had tilted over, with my head actually on the bed. She said I snored."

"And she didn't wake you up?"

"She felt sorry for me. I think she also figured I'd be a better doctor if I were a little more rested. So she let me sleep there, and even kept other people out so I wouldn't be disturbed."

"I think my worst was the elevator. I got on, leaned back in the corner, and apparently rode up and down for fifteen minutes before somebody was kind enough to lead me off." He looked none the worse for the wear, she thought, still trying to make a casual observation. In fact, for all the hours he'd put in, he looked rather amazing. "Can I get you something, Michael? To eat, or drink?"

"Damn it, Sarah! I can get it myself! What the hell makes you think I need or want you to wait on me? I mean, who the hell do you think you are to me?"

That was a mood swing she hadn't expected out of Michael. His mood changed so drastically, so quickly, it took Sarah a moment to realize that it had actually happened, and when that finally sank in, she was left wondering why. What was so dark in Michael that made him so defensive? "I wasn't suggesting that you *couldn't* help yourself, Michael." She struggled to tamp back her own flare of temper. "But I'm at the end of my break and you're at the beginning of yours, so I thought I'd do the polite thing and—"

"And what?" he snapped again. "Save me steps? *Poor Michael. Look at the way he limps.* Is that it? My leg makes me incapable of taking care of myself? Is that how you see it, because if it is, save the pity, Sarah. I don't need it. Not from anyone, and especially not from you!"

Well, this was certainly a little hotbed of something she'd stumbled into. Problem was, she couldn't hang around and find out what it was about. Duty called and medical emergencies took precedent over bad moods. "Good thing I don't generally give pity," she said, standing up. "And just so you'll know, Michael, I'd have made the same offer even if you didn't limp. Call me crazy that way, but I do like helping people when I can, and whether or not you want to admit it, you looked like…and still do look like…you need some help. But not from me. I'm out of here. Back to work. If you want something, get it yourself!" She headed toward the door but stopped before she got there, then turned back to face him. "You know what, Michael? We all have problems right now, and while yours may legitimately be worse than most of the others, it's not right to take it out on me…or anyone else who's simply trying to be kind. I know you're in charge here, but I'd suggest you get your bad mood under control before you come back to work because none of us needs to deal with that along with everything else going on." Harsh words, but she was glad she'd said them because he needed to hear them. He could bask in his damn bad mood another time, but right now he had more important things to think about.

As Sarah stepped into the passage, Michael let out a frustrated sigh. "Don't go," he managed, pushing himself part way up to look at her.

"Why shouldn't I?" she asked, without turning around. She had so many feelings swirling around....anger, hurt, frustration. *Confusion*. They seemed to do so well together in so many ways, her and Michael, yet there was always an intense wariness between them, one that neither of them had penetrated yet, and she wasn't sure what to do about it. Or if she even wanted to try doing something. He wasn't the only one with problems and complications in his life, and if they hadn't been in such close proximity, she would have left. Right then. Left the ship, no looking back. Well, that wasn't an option, was it? She wasn't going to jump overboard, and the doctor in her compelled her to be here, with Michael, to take care of these people. So that was it— no choices.

"Look, Sarah, I think I owe you an explanation," he continued. "And an apology for being so bad-tempered with you just now."

"No, you don't owe me a thing," she said. Finally, she turned to face him. "Except civility."

"People patronize me. Treat me like I lost my intelligence with my leg."

She wasn't surprised, but that still wasn't a good enough reason for his attitude toward her. *Who the hell do you think you are to me?* She'd thought she was his friend. Maybe a little more. Silly her. "Maybe they do, and I'm sorry for that, but I'm not like that, Michael, and you know it. And I resent being the one you pick on because you're feeling bad."

"Look, could we pretend that I never came into the room and made a total idiot of myself?"

She did want to. But the things he'd said had cut so deeply

she needed time to figure it out. "The deed's done, Michael. But go ahead and pretend anything you want to, if it's easier for you."

Propping his head up on the armrest, Michael studied Sarah from that position for a moment, without making any effort to get up. "You're an odd woman, Sarah Collins."

"In a good or a bad way?"

"I don't think there's anything about you that could be odd in a bad way."

"So I should take that as a compliment, that I'm odd in a good way? A sincere compliment, I hope, seeing that you're trying to redeem yourself from being a total idiot."

"You're straightforward," he said. "More so than anybody else I know, except Ina. Most people won't even mention my disability, yet you seem to have some insight. And some gall to ague with a cripple, which, I might add, most people won't do."

"In other words, you beat them up and they let you?"

"I don't beat them up, as you think. Most of the time I get better results beating myself up."

She wanted to ask. Dear God, she wanted to ask. But there wasn't time. "You said I had insight into your disability? Remember, I had a husband with terminal melanoma, so I suppose that did give me some insight. Oh, and in case I hadn't mentioned it before, after Kerry died I got myself engaged to a man with leukemia. More insight there." Lots of it, for a very long time.

"Did he…?"

"He didn't die, but we didn't make it." She forced a half-smile, then left the room. There would be time for talking later. If Michael wanted to talk. If *she* wanted to talk.

"I'm sorry," he called after her. "Please, Sarah. Forgive me."

She turned back to the room to accept his apology, just in time to see Michael nod off. No snoring, though. The patient whose bed he'd slept on all those years ago must have lied about that. Not that it mattered, because when would she and Michael ever share a bed?

CHAPTER NINE

"You let me sleep for two hours!" Michael said, as Sarah sailed past him to admit the next patient.

The toll had now risen to seventy-six, and even though most of them were a long way from being critical, she was past the point of being tired. Her feet hurt. So did her head, her shoulders, her back. As well as everything else. But she was running on pure adrenalin now, so wired that even if she'd had the chance to sleep, she probably couldn't.

"You needed it, and we were slow. We're keeping those patients with the minor symptoms to confined to their cabins with instructions to check back in with us if their symptoms get worse. And I'm not patronizing you because of your disability. Just giving you my medical opinion." She flashed him a grin. "Which, in this case, was valid. You look better."

"I don't get you, Sarah. You didn't want to practice medicine so you quit it, yet when you're given the opportunity to work again you blossom."

"Sometimes it's not so much about what we want to do as what we have to do." Before he could ask what that meant, she turned down a side corridor leading to the small lab area and disappeared into the cubbyhole where Helen Weinstein, a seventy-something retired lab technician, was busy examining blood samples. "Anything yet?" Sarah asked.

"It's a nice lab, very modern, but limited in its scope. I'm seeing a run of elevated white cells, elevated blood sugars, but nothing really significant other than that. And I don't have the equipment to test for many of the specific conditions I'd like to. But I've got some bacterial cultures incubating and maybe that will tell us more. Unfortunately, they take time."

"Do you think it could be bacterial? All along we've been going on the assumption that it's some kind of virus, but if it's bacterial that would make the way we're treating this entirely different." She did a mental check of all the various symptoms they were seeing, and while there was some commonality, there wasn't enough to be conclusive. But the possibility that this could be bacterial did raise some interesting questions, such as where was the point of origin? In a virus it didn't matter. One person got it, they coughed or sneezed and spread it to another. It was contagious from person to person. Bacteria weren't contagious like that, so if this mystery illness wasn't being transmitted that way…

"What if it's not viral?" she asked Michael a few minutes later as they passed in the hall, practically bumping into each other they were both moving so fast in opposite directions.

"Then we don't have enough broad-spectrum antibiotics to treat everybody who's ill, and we'll have to evacuate them to a hospital. What makes you think it's not a virus?"

"Something Helen Weinstein said."

"Who?"

"The purple-hat lady who's running the lab now. She said she's not seeing much of a commonality in the blood samples. Nothing is really popping out at her and she doesn't have the right equipment to get too specific. But she's growing some cultures, and I think that's certainly something to think about. Food-borne and water-borne bacteria occur all the time."

"In the form of gastric upset normally."

"Except most of our patients have respiratory symptoms to some degree, and practically none of them have gastrointestinal problems. And it's causing system-wide problems…blood in the urine, abnormal blood sugar. I just saw one patient with an elevated blood sugar who swears she's not diabetic, yet her blood sugar is extremely high. So I did an A-one-C—" a test averaging out blood sugar levels "—and she's normal. In fact, she's perfect. But her blood sugar's hovering at three hundred and fifty right now, so something caused it to get that high."

"And you're inclined to believe your patient isn't simply over-indulging, like so many of the others are?"

"I'm inclined to believe her."

"Just like I'm inclined to believe Reese Allen didn't lie on his physical exam to work on the ship when he said he had no history of heart disease, yet he's just a tick shy of a heart attack."

Sarah frowned for a moment, then her frown line changed into a more thoughtful expression. "A couple of years ago Cameron and I had a patient who complained about lingering flu. She said she'd had it for a month and couldn't shake it, and she decided it was time to see a doctor. She didn't have a regular doctor so she called us to schedule herself in, but she missed her appointment, and I got word that she'd been admitted to the hospital in a critical condition. Her symptoms…" Sarah's eyes widened. "They were all over the place, Michael. But we never saw her and, to be honest, I didn't give it a thought as she never requested that either of us take her case while she was hospitalized."

"Well, most of our patients do have flu-like symptoms," he said. "Among other things. Do you think anyone might remember that case you mentioned?"

"My ex-fiancé." It wouldn't be an awkward phone call because there was no animosity between them, but talking to Cameron again would bring back memories of things she'd have rather forgotten. Dark days in her life she wasn't particularly proud of. "I guess it's time to give him a call, isn't it?" she said drearily.

"I can do it, Sarah. I know it's not always easy, facing people from your past. I've got a few of those ghosts myself."

"No, it's not easy facing the people you let down, is it?"

Michael was quiet for a moment, then he forced himself to speak. "You're being too hard on yourself," he said, his voice unusually strained. "I'm sure that whatever happened between the two of you isn't as bad as you think it is."

Spoken like a man who hadn't come to terms with his ghosts. Her heart did go out to him. It was hard, living with something terrible in your past. Not standing by someone she'd loved while he'd been experiencing the worst tragedy he'd ever faced, and needed that support to help get them through, was her ghost. Along with all the emotional distance she'd built. "What happened between the two of us was worse than you could imagine," she said, as she walked away.

It took ten minutes before the call went through to Cameron. He was a small-town doctor now, married to a veterinarian, and from what she'd heard he was thriving in every way possible. Marriage and fatherhood agreed with him, and she heard that the instant his cheery voice burst onto the line with, "Sarah! It's great to hear from you again. How are you doing? I understand you've been on an extended holiday."

"And I understand that you've got quite the life going for yourself," she said, avoiding any talk of herself.

"Everything I've always wanted. Health's good, too. Full remission, and I'm feeling better than I have in years."

She was happy for him. So happy, in fact, that tears began to slide down her cheeks. Cameron had never been bitter, had never held any feelings of anger toward her, and she could hear that in him now. He was such a wonderful man. He deserved a wonderful life. "You deserve all the good things you've gotten," she said, fighting to hold her voice steady as she swiped at the tears with the back of her hand.

From behind her, Michael gave her a tissue.

"Look, I'd love to catch up with everything you're doing, and maybe we can in the future, but I'm in the middle of a medical situation right now, and I need some advice."

"You've gone back into medicine?" Cameron asked. "Sarah, I'm so glad you finally realized that nothing was your fault. Not my illness, not the way I put off treatment, not the way we turned out. I've felt terrible, knowing you'd quit the practice and sold your half of it because of me, but now that you're back…where are you practicing, by the way?"

She closed her eyes, picturing Cameron. Just a shade shorter than Michael, he was muscular but not large, and he had dark brown hair, but not as dark as Michael's, with… Funny, she couldn't remember the color of Cameron's eyes any longer. Michael's were a haunting dark brown, but were Cameron's brown too, or green perhaps? How could something she'd seen so often have simply slipped from her mind? But the more she thought about Cameron now, the more his image blurred until he was indistinguishable from Michael. Then he was Michael, in her mind. "I'm not exactly back in a practice, but I'm helping out in a cruise ship's hospital, and we've got an outbreak of something I thought you might remember from a couple of years ago."

Cameron chuckled. "I always picture you more as staid. You know, someone who wanted an orderly life, personally and professionally. Wouldn't have ever guessed you'd wind up as a ship's doctor, but if that's what you like, I'm happy for you, Sarah. Now, tell me about this outbreak."

Sarah went into details for the next several minutes, telling Cameron everything she knew, which wasn't nearly enough. But when she was finished, she held her breath, hoping he remembered their similar case. "It was odd," he said, "because it didn't come to us in an outbreak, and normally legionnella, or legionnaires' disease, comes in an outbreak where numbers of people are affected. Like what you've got going on there. Without the tests I can't say for sure, but it sure sounds the same to me."

"Oh, my God," she whispered, a new sense of dread coming over her now. Legionnaires' disease could be fatal, yet it was also highly treatable if caught in time. She'd never treated a case herself, but now all the varying symptoms were making sense to her. Incubation period was right, the ship's conditions were certainly favorable to it... "That's not what I wanted to hear."

With those words, Michael stepped up behind her, slipping a steadying arm around her waist as Sarah said thanks and goodbye. After she'd hung up the phone, she stayed in his partial embrace. "Legionnaires' disease, if it's full-blown, and Pontiac fever if it's not." One would require strict medical treatment, and the other would run its course in a matter of a few days. Both were the same illness, but they attacked in differing degrees, hence the different names. The only good news in this whole mess was that legionnaires' was not communicable from person to person.

"So now we X-ray everybody to see who has pneumonia and who doesn't, get the ones who do on antibiotics, keep treating the various other problems people are having, and hope no one else comes down with it."

"And find the source," Sarah said, relieved that the medical mystery was possibly solved but dreading the next phase of what they were going to have to face. Right about now a nice little secluded booth in a dimly lit karaoke bar sounded awfully good, and she wondered if she and Michael would ever meet there again. Probably not, considering the way they'd been last time they'd sat together in a dark booth. "Let me go and see who, among our purple-hat nurses, has experience in taking X-rays."

There came a point when the body just gave out, and Michael had reached that point finally. He hated the fact that he didn't

have all his endurance back yet. He'd spent months in reha-
bilitation, then months after that working alone, retraining
himself in all the strenuous physical activities that had once
come so easily, but now, when it mattered, he wasn't up to
it. He had to take a break. Even after that two-hour nap
sixteen hours ago, he had to take a break. And he was disgusted with himself for that.

OK. So he was weak. He admitted it. The prosthesis had
to come off for a while. No getting around it, unless he
wanted to cause himself even more trouble. But, damn it, why
now? They had just over a hundred patients, the preliminary
diagnosis stage was still in progress, the tests and X-rays
were under way, and he needed to be there to make sure his
hospital ran as efficiently as it could, given the fact that he
was the only staff physician left healthy. But he had to walk
out. Had to turn his hospital over to Sarah and Dr Emma
Needham, one of the purple-hat ladies, and limp away.

*Had to go off and take a nap, just like that day when he'd
done the same thing to his medics and got them killed.*

Even now, thinking about it made his pulse quicken. Made
him break out in a cold sweat. "No distractions," he warned
himself, forcing himself to think about the technicians who
would shortly come aboard to find the source of the bacterium
and establish its nature once and for all. He mentally tracked
the next hours to come. He would take a short nap, then make
a transport manifest for his sickest patients. After that he
would assess those with the milder form of the illness and give
them the option of leaving or staying. Yes, that was the course
of action he'd be taking, and as for the rest of the cruise…
Actually, at this point he didn't give a damn about what
happened. As far as he was concerned, they could turn the ship
around and head back to Florida, to their port of origin, and
end this cruise. Most likely, that would be his recommenda-
tion at a meeting called for the ship's senior personnel in a
couple of hours since, as of yet, they had no idea where the

bacteria were multiplying. It could be anywhere…ventila-
tion shafts, showers, hot tubs. Anywhere with a water source,
which meant it was still a danger for all the guests.

Too tired to remove his clothes, or anything else, Michael
slumped down into his bed and simply stared up at the
ceiling. Sleep wasn't eluding him as much as he was fighting
it off. He wanted to feel the ache for a while. It reminded him
of all the things that had turned his life over, and he did need
to be reminded from time to time. Some of that beating up
he did to himself. Brent Mullavey, Greg Warren…his friends.
Men he'd counted on. Men who'd counted on him. Their
images were always on the edge of his mind, where they
needed to be. He should have let go of them months ago. The
military doctors who'd taken care of him had told him it was
time to do that. But he couldn't…

"Four hours now, and I'm worried," Sarah said, as the ship's
maintenance man pulled out his master key and inserted it
into the lock on Michael's door. Michael had gone to take a
break four hours ago and hadn't come back. To be honest,
she'd been so busy she hadn't really noticed how long he'd
been was gone until Ina had pointed it out. After that, she'd
been in quite a panic, trying to find someone to come open
his cabin door.

"He's going to hate this." Ina's voice was more worried
than wary as she huddled behind Sarah, gripping her medical
bag so tightly her knuckles were turning white. "Mike is a
great guy, but he hates intrusion into his personal space. He's
private that way. Doesn't want people interfering." Worry
changed to panic on Ina's face as the maintenance man
fumbled with his keys, trying to get the lock to open. "Can't
you hurry?" she snapped.

Sarah's own worry was evident in the way she balled her
fist and struck the doorframe each time Bruno, the mainte-

nance man, failed to open the door. Then finally it gave and they were in. Sarah first, followed by Ina, then by Bruno.

"Michael!" Sarah called out in her mad rush across the cabin. Ina ran forward too, but Bruno, who might not have recognized a critically ill patient, did recognize the fact that an unresponsive patient wasn't good.

"Can I go get something for you?" he asked.

Sarah dropped down onto the bed next to Michael and immediately felt for his pulse. Fast, weak. And he was burning up with fever. "Go to the hospital and have someone bring a gurney down here," she said. "Tell them stat. They'll know what that means."

Ina, who was in the process of strapping a blood-pressure cuff to Michael's arm, cast Bruno an impatient glance as he hesitated for a moment to watch what they were doing. "Stat means immediately," she said, her voice razor-sharp.

"Legionnaires'," Sarah said on her way to the bathroom to fetch a basin of cool water. "I need him set up with an IV so we can get an antibiotic into him immediately. Acetaminophen, too, to bring down his fever. Can you go get that? I'd rather get it started here before we move him."

"Blood pressure's low," Ina reported. "But not abnormally. And I'm on my way to get the IV set-up. Does he need oxygen?"

"Probably not," she called from the bathroom. "His breathing seems fine for now. Wouldn't hurt to support him once we get him to the hospital, though." Sarah returned to Michael's bedside, carrying a basin of water after Ina left the cabin, immediately stripped off his shirt and applied a washcloth to his head, then one to his chest. Nice mat of soft, dark hair, she thought as started to removing the rest of his clothing to help him cool off. "Somehow I'd thought that the first time I saw you naked would be something other than this." Unzipping his white uniform pants, she slid them down over his legs. "Actually, that night at Evangeline's, I would have been very happy to see you naked, maybe in the broom closet or even under the table."

She paused for a moment, looking at his prosthesis. It was the first time she'd seen it, and she was amazed by the technology. She'd witnessed the working of a trans-tibial prosthesis on several occasions in her medical practice, but seeing it now on someone she knew, someone she cared about... Blinking hard, Sarah shook all that out of her mind as she removed his shoes, then his prosthetic leg. "I'll bet you're thinking I'm going to remove your underwear," she said, draping a sheet over his body for modesty's sake. "But I won't. At least, not while you're unconscious like this."

Would she have been so bold as to say these things to him if he'd been conscious? Probably not. That wasn't in her nature. Of course, what she'd done with him at Evangeline's wasn't in her nature either. But she'd been thinking these things, and more, for a while, and talking to Michael did make her less nervous as she examined him.

Another check of his pulse revealed nothing different from the first time. It was a little off but not dangerously so. And listening to his chest really didn't reveal any congestion, which was good, even though pneumonia was always a worry where legionella bacteria was concerned. Yet here he was right now, another case of non-specific symptoms, which meant the bacteria could be attacking just about any of his systems in ways she couldn't detect under these circumstances. That scared her, not just for Michael, but for everyone on board. "Look, Michael, I know this probably isn't the best time to iron out our differences but, to be honest, I probably wouldn't even say this if you could hear me. Or maybe you can. Who knows?" She laughed nervously as she sat down on the bed next to him. "But that night at Evangeline's...I'm not usually like that. Normally I'm pretty reserved, but you're so right about the chemistry. It's there. We've got it. To me, though, it goes beyond chemistry, which is why I would have… Well, what I'm trying to say is that, for me, it takes more than chemistry. At least, under normal circumstances. And I'm trying to figure it out…figure out what made me act that way. But I don't want you to think that I'm loose, or anything like that, because I'm not. It's just that I think I might be…" No, she couldn't say the words to him, not even when he was unconscious. Couldn't tell him she might be falling in love. That was too complicated, even for a man in his condition. And especially for herself.

Sarah pushed a stray lock of damp hair from his forehead, dipped the washcloth in the basin of water she'd set at the side of the bed, then reapplied it to his forehead. "Not that anything between us could ever happen," she continued. "But I want you to know that just because I shut people out of my life, it doesn't mean that I'm not normal in those ways. *Because I am*. You proved that." More than she'd thought anybody could.

She laid her fingers to his pulse again, not because there was anything she could do so much as she simply wanted to make contact with him. *Physical* contact to reassure him, on some level, that she was there with him. "You're going to be fine, Michael. I don't know what you went though that got you injured so badly, but I promise that I'll see you though this." She had no other choice. Whether or not she wanted to admit it, she loved him, and if there was one thing she was good at, it was standing by the men she loved. In the physical sense, anyway.

So maybe he had to hear that. Maybe she had to go against everything she'd held back from herself and tell him. Because, God forbid, if he died… No! She wouldn't think like that. Wouldn't make the same terrible mistakes she'd made before either.

Suddenly it was all so clear to her. Mistakes from the past…mistakes she wouldn't repeat. She had to do this because she didn't want the regrets, and in a life filled with them what she felt for Michael wouldn't be turned into another. Bending down to his ear, she whispered, "I do love you, Michael. I don't know what that means yet, but I think I've loved you almost from the moment I collapsed in your arms."

It felt good. Amazingly good. And right. Sitting back, pleased with her decision, she was dipping the washcloth in the basin to sponge off his chest again when Ina ran into the cabin, followed by a brigade of purple-hat volunteers pushing the gurney. Because Michael was a large, robust man, it took every woman in the room to lift him onto the gurney, but once they had, they whisked him away to the hospital, leaving Sarah behind to close up his cabin. As she started to pull the door shut, she took another look at his prosthetic leg. It didn't make him less of a man, didn't make him anything other than who he was. And it didn't matter to her. But she had a disturbing feeling that it mattered to Michael in more ways than she could understand. Maybe more than he could understand, too.

In a life full of ups and downs with her past relationships, she was fully aware of why she held back from getting involved in another one again. But was she looking at the reason Michael held himself back? That might have been part of it, she decided. Somewhere deep down, though, he had other demons. She was sure of it. Someone with her fair share of demons knew the symptoms when she saw them.

"Michael, you're in the hospital."

Of course he was. That's where he worked, and it was time to get up from his nap and get back to it.

"You're going to be just fine. Your temperature's come down now, your vital signs are stable, and there's no sign of any permanent damage."

Damn, he hated taking naps. Normally he felt worse afterwards than he had before. That's why he didn't nap very often, because he always came out of it feeling like hell. Like he did now.

"They found the source of the legionella bacteria. It wasn't on the ship after all. It seems that the hotel where so many of the passengers and crew stayed the night before the cruise launched had the bacteria cultivating in their ventilation system. Everybody who stayed there breathed it in."

He'd stayed there, but apparently he'd escaped the effects. Opening his eyes to Sarah, Michael wondered how she'd gotten into his cabin. "How long did you let me sleep this time?" he muttered, raising his hand to visor his eyes from the bright light overhead and for the first time noticing the IV in his wrist. "What's this?" he sputtered, now trying to sit up.

Sarah laid a gentle hand on his shoulder to keep him down. "Normal saline now, with a piggyback of an antibiotic in another three hours."

It didn't make sense. He'd gone to take a nap. Just a few minutes off his feet then back to work. But he'd heard Sarah's voice waft in and out. He remembered that. Had it been in his dream? And why the IV? "What happened?" he asked, fighting to remember, to clear the fog that had settled over his brain.

"You got sick. The cultures were positive for legionnaires', and you came down with it. You've been sick with low-grade pneumonia these past couple of days, lapsing in and out of consciousness. But the pneumonia's cleared and you're on the mend."

"Am I still on the ship?"

"You're in Miami. You were transported with the other patients. Everything's under control now."

Under control. He was lying flat on his back in a hospital again after he'd vowed that no matter what happened to him he'd never go back to another hospital as a patient. "When can I leave?" he asked, turning slightly sideways to take in his surroundings. It was a private room, not a critical-care unit. That was good.

"If you keep responding to treatment, maybe in a week or so."

"You've stayed here with me the whole time?"

"I promised I would."

He vaguely remembered that promise. Or he thought he did. "And everybody's fine? All the people who contracted…" Glancing up at her face, he knew the answer she was fighting desperately to hide. "How many?" he choked.

"We can talk about that later."

"No. We can talk about it now. How many people did we lose?"

Drawing in a long, ragged breath, Sarah took hold of Michael's hand. "Just one. I'm sorry, Michael, but it was…"

"Reese Allen. The bacteria lodged in his heart, didn't it?"

She nodded. "The medical examiner said that he did have a weak heart and that was the easiest thing for the bacteria to attack. He also said he didn't believe Dr Allen was aware of his heart defect."

"And I came close to dying?"

Sarah nodded again. "Because you've had so many surgeries in the recent past. They weakened your system and the legionella bacteria love to attack a weakened system."

He didn't know what to say, and even if he had, he didn't have the energy. So he shut his eyes and drifted back to sleep, but not before something flashed through his mind. *I've loved you almost from the moment I collapsed in your arms.* Had he dreamt that? Dreamt that in Sarah's voice? "Go away," he murmured as he drifted off. "Go away, Sarah."

He was sick, grumpy, probably frustrated by the inconvenience of being confined to bed, which was why she wasn't taking his mood personally. In her experience she'd dealt with much worse. So taking a break was good, and in a while, after she returned to Michael's room, maybe he'd feel better. Maybe he'd be in a better mood, too.

Both Ina and Martha had been at her side almost constantly these past days. They'd become friends she'd never expected to find in a life she'd never expected to find. Bright spots in so much uncertainty.

"I think he's waking up again," the nurse on duty said three hours later as she poked her head into the doctors' lounge, where Sarah had practically taken up residence this past week.

"Thank you." It was tough, not knowing whether she should go back to him now or leave him alone for a while longer. The last couple of times he'd woken up he'd just told her to go away. Nothing else. And, frankly, that's what she expected this time. Ina said it was because he wasn't ready to face the truth. But was it the truth he feared? Or did he fear her? Did he really love her, the way he'd said he did every time he'd woken up these past few days. He'd told her, he'd told Ina and Martha, he'd told any number of nurses… But that had been delirium, and, as much as she wanted to believe it was something else, she wasn't going to allow herself to believe it. He was a very sick man. That's all it was.

But it had been nice to hear, nevertheless. Now she wondered if he remembered some of the things he'd babbled, and that scared him if they were true. Or made him feel guilty if they were not.

Why were the deepest personal feelings, like loving someone, the hardest to admit to? Why were they the ones that scared you the most? Rather than making life better, they became a complication, which didn't seem right. Vulnerability, she decided. The hardest thing to do was to make yourself vulnerable to someone else. But it was also the nicest, because that's where the true bond started—a bond she'd thought about over these days sitting at Michael's bedside. A bond she truly wanted with him. But now she was scared, too. Which took her right back to her original question. *Why were the deepest personal feelings, like loving someone, the hardest to admit to?*

"You should go to him," Martha prompted. "He needs you now more than ever."

"And be kicked out again."

"It's not personal, sweetie. You know that."

Sarah signed wearily. "But what it if is? I think he either remembers some of the things he said…"

"Or he's afraid of some of the things *you* said. Is that what's bothering you? That you opened yourself up to him so much? Made yourself vulnerable?"

"You heard?" How could that be? Yes, she'd told him she loved him, told him that several times. But she'd been alone. So how could Martha have known?"

Martha chuckled. "No, I didn't eavesdrop on your conversations with him. But it's in your face, Sarah, in the way you look at him, the way you respond to him, the way you touch him when you're taking care of him. So, tell me, how could you *not* sit at the bedside of the man you love without telling him that you love him?"

Martha was right about that. She couldn't. "Do you think he heard me, and he doesn't want to deal with me now?"

"I think he doesn't know *how* to deal with you, sweetie. He's a lot like you, the way he tries to keep to himself and push everybody away. If you want my opinion, though, I think you pierced his armor and he doesn't know what to do about it. The way he pierced yours. Only he changed the rules by getting sick. He needed you and you were forced to give in to your feelings for him in order to help him." She smiled. "Which gives you an advantage he hasn't had. It's amazing, isn't it, how sometimes the worst situations bring out the best truths?"

Truths she didn't know what to do with. Sarah took two steps toward the door, then turned back to Martha. "Falling in love shouldn't be so hard. I thought if I ever did it again it would be…I don't know. Maybe without problems? You know, something simple."

"If it's without problems, or simple, then it's not true love. And what you feel for Michael is true love, isn't it?"

"True love. That can't work itself out." She shook her head. "It's so complicated, Martha. I don't handle true love as well as it should be handled. I let people down, do the wrong things for what I believe are the right reasons, and end up just making a mess of it. I'm not sure I've got it in me to do it again."

"Which is why you keep to yourself. Not trying is easier than taking a plunge into the great unknown. Well, I don't know what happened with your late husband, sweetie, or that other gentleman you told me about, but from what I've observed with the way you've been with Doctor Sloan, I'd say you've done everything perfectly and the greatest unknown should be how you'll survive without him *and not* how you'll let him into your life. I think you're the hardest critic of yourself, even though you've got no call to be that way now. Yet words aren't going to make you believe that, Sarah. It's going to take time, and patience, and the love of a good man that lets your heart truly trust again…and that includes trusting yourself. So you'd better go to him while he's awake and tell him you're not going anywhere."

Sound advice, except running away would have been the easiest thing to do. Leave, and never come back. Her heart was fully committed, though. And she was so tired of running. So very tired…

"Michael," she said quietly as she slipped into his room and took her regular seat by the side of his bed.

His eyes fluttered open to her. "Have I told you that I love you, Sarah? Have I told you yet?"

"Yes," she said, realizing he was on his way down again. "And I love you, too." Her love wasn't the blear that comes from a spiking fever either.

"Good," he murmured, as he slipped away. "I'm glad you do."

* * *

"He's gone?" Sarah stared at the empty bed, still not believing what she was seeing. "Michael's gone?" He wasn't ready. Wasn't well enough yet.

"Checked himself out an hour ago," the nurse said. "AMA." Against medical advice. "We tried to convince him to stay, but he refused, and there was nothing we could do to stop him. Dr Sloan called a private hire to take him, then left."

She couldn't believe it! "Do you know where he went?"

The nurse shook her head. "All he said was that he'd consult a doctor when he arrived at his destination. No word where that destination is, though."

She'd been gone four hours. *That's all.* Four lousy hours because she'd needed to take a walk, get some fresh air. So she'd gone back to the hotel in which she hadn't slept, taken a shower, then had a stroll on the beach. Four hours, and he'd taken full advantage of the time! "How was he, physically?"

"Weak, but coherent."

He'd been coherent for the past day and a half. Coherent and totally unresponsive to her. Every time she'd gone to his room he'd spent his time staring out the window or faking sleep. She'd known he was improving, and she'd hoped that his attitude would improve too, but apparently that had been nothing more than wishful thinking on her part. Obviously, he'd planned on leaving, on walking away from her the first chance he got.

"He did leave you this note." The nurse handed Sarah a sealed envelope, but Sarah didn't want to open it there because she knew what was inside would make her go to pieces. She wanted to be alone for that. Alone, the way she should have stayed all along.

Sitting on a bench in the lush tropical garden outside the hotel, with the scent of gardenias and salt water in the air, Sarah stared at the ocean just across the way for nearly twenty minutes before she finally tucked her little finger under the envelope's flap and ripped it open. Inside she saw the white

sheet of paper, and it took her another ten minutes to pull it
out and open it up.

Dear Sarah, it started.

She drew in a deep breath, bracing herself for the pain that
was inevitable.

*Sometimes, these past few days, I've heard myself
telling you, telling everyone else that I love you, and I
do. I want you to know that it wasn't crazy talk from a
man who was out of his head. You said you loved me
almost from the moment you collapsed in my arms and
I've held onto that through my delirium. And, yes, it's
true what they say about how some people, when
they're unconscious, can hear what's going on around
them, because I did hear you. Everything you said to
me. And here's the funny thing. I fell in love with you
almost at the same time you did, when you collapsed
in my arms. You looked up at me with so much trust,
and you were so beautiful, how could I not?*

*You had such a wall around you, though, which kept
you safe. But it kept me safe, too, from the very same
things you didn't want in your life. Except we had that
chemistry, didn't we? Nothing to deny there. Which
made it so tough for me, because I can't have a relationship with you…and it has nothing to do with you.*

*You have such a good, kind heart, Sarah. There's so
much to give deep inside you, and I would love, with
all my heart, to be the one to take what you want to give,
but I can't. My life isn't worked out, and I can't drag
you into it.*

*You need to live your life for yourself now, Sarah. I
don't think you've done much of that because you are
such a dutiful, faithful woman. But to the wrong man
this time. Please know that I won't stop loving you*

even though, with a small piece of my heart, I do hope that you can find it in yourself to stop loving me.

Let your heart tell you what to do. Listen, Sarah. It won't let you down.

Too numb to cry, too numb to even breathe, Sarah stared at the ocean for another hour, clutching Michael's letter to her chest, before she finally got up and returned to her hotel room. Then she packed, and finally went home to Boston. Home, for the first time in a year.

CHAPTER TEN

It WAS a nice cabin, and she'd been sitting in her parked rental car, down the road from it and out of view, for the past hour, trying to gather up the courage to do this. It had been a month now, and she had to. He'd had his space, she'd had hers, and with every breath she'd drawn during those long, empty days she'd come to realize just how much she wanted him in her space. That's all there was, and if Michael was worth loving the way she did, he was worth fighting for. This time it was different, though. Her future wasn't slipping down a drain the way it had while Kerry had been dying, or while her relationship with Cameron had been ending. With Michael she had no future unless she went after it. And she wanted to go after it. Give herself that chance to fight for it and, if nothing else this time, walk away knowing she'd done everything she could.

But that scared her, because she didn't count on him having a change of heart. And this would be the very last time. If he succeeded in pushing her away this time, he'd never let her get near him again. She was sure of it.

He loved her, though. She knew that more than she knew just about anything else. Michael Sloan did love her. Which was what made this the most important thing she'd ever done in her life. So now it was time to prepare herself for all the things that had to be said, and do whatever it would take to fight for *them*. For Michael and herself as a couple.

Gritting her teeth with the resolve she'd been working on this past month, Sarah turned the key in the ignition and headed down the road after what she wanted.

"I like it here," she said, stepping up to the porch rail where he was perched, looking out over the lake. He looked good. Rested. Healthy again. "It's peaceful."

"It's not mine," he said flatly. "I don't need a home, with the way I live. Borrowing one is just fine. Better than owning, as you don't have any permanent ties."

She chuckled on the outside even though she winced internally. He was so hard now. Pulled so far into his emotional scars she wasn't sure she knew how to break through. "You sound like me. No need for permanent roots. Just go wherever the urge takes you." Except her urge took her only one place now. No matter how this turned out, her days of wandering were over.

He didn't respond to that. Neither did he make a move toward her. Didn't even look at her, but, then, she didn't expect him to. Although she'd really hoped for something else...open arms, maybe? It would have been a nice start, she thought on a sad note. "How are you, Michael?" she finally asked, breaking the icy silence between them. "I've been worried." He hadn't returned her phone calls, but she'd never quit calling so he'd had to expect this...expect that at some point she'd come here. She'd half expected to find that he'd moved on without leaving a forwarding address. So maybe his still being here was a good sign. She desperately hoped so.

"Why the hell can't people just leave me alone? Did it ever occur to you that I'm out here at this lake, all alone, cut off from society, because I want to be?"

"Actually, yes. It did. When Ina told me where you were, she also mentioned that you didn't want to be bothered. Which is why I came."

"To bother me?"

"Yes, to bother you. Because I know some of your isolation has to do with me, and I don't want it to. So I had to come find you, to tell you…"

"What?" he snapped, finally turning to face her. "That you love me? Because I already know that. So what can you tell me that I *don't* already know?"

The pain was so stark in his eyes it shocked her, and broke her heart. But this time she couldn't quit, couldn't back away like she had before. Couldn't let him bully her into backing away. "I know what it's like to live with a different image of yourself, to have something you counted on taken away."

"My leg?" He barked a bitter laugh. "You don't know anything, Sarah. Not a damned thing!" Spinning away, he walked through the French windows back into the lodge, and was halfway up the stairs by the time she'd caught up with him.

"I do know, Michael. I know what it's like to watch the man you love lose his body image by bits and pieces. To go from a large, athletic man who competed in marathons to one who weighed barely a hundred pounds, who'd lost all his hair, whose skin just hung on his bones. I lived with that, and loved a man who was going through it. So don't tell me that I don't know, because I do."

"It's not about my leg," he insisted, but this time his voice wasn't so sharp. Turning to face Sarah, he stared down at her but didn't attempt to come back down the stairs. "And sometimes it gets to the point where body image just doesn't matter any more."

"It never does, Michael. More than once, when he didn't know that I could see him, I saw Kerry stand at the mirror and look at himself. And cry. The tears weren't for the cancer, but for the losses he could see in that damned mirror. Inside he was still the same man, but on the outside he was ravaged by an illness he couldn't control, and the visual reminder was as much a part of what he was dealing with as was his cancer.

Maybe even more, since it was a constant harbinger even on the days when he wasn't feeling so bad.

"And I wasn't there for him, Michael. Oh, in the physical sense I never left his side. But there's something more…the things that needed saying. Things he needed to say that I *couldn't* hear. Things I wanted to say that I was afraid to. Which is why I'm here. There are things I need to say now, things you need to hear, and I won't do to you what I did to Kerry." She fought back a strangled sob, angry that she was reduced to tears. She didn't want to be because it made her vulnerable, and for Michael's sake she couldn't be vulnerable in this. He needed her strength…her complete strength. A strength that had faltered for Kerry, and even for Cameron.

Bracing herself, she fought off the tears stinging her eyes, threatening to spill. She wouldn't cry, wouldn't give way to her emotions. *Not this time.* "So you can run away, Michael, but I'll just follow you."

"I'm sorry," he said, his voice barely above a whisper. "I don't want to hurt you, Sarah. I never wanted to do that. But you don't understand. I just…just can't do this."

"Then make me understand. You owe me that much, Michael. If you love me, like you said you do, then you owe it to me to make me understand."

"Maybe I do."

The resignation in his voice was thick, but not as thick as the lines creased into his face now. Michael looked like he'd aged ten years in the past few minutes and she couldn't help but think that her coming here had caused that.

"But even if I do make you understand, I still can't make it right for us, Sarah. What's broken is inside me, and it can't be fixed. I've tried, but nothing changes. And words are only words. They don't make the deeds go away."

She swallowed hard, still looking up the stairs at him. "After Kerry died, when I was engaged to Cameron, he put me off. I knew something was wrong with him…as his fiancée, as a doctor, I could see it. It showed in every way I looked at him, but yet when I mentioned it to him, asked him if he was feeling well, asked him if he'd had a physical check-up lately, he put me off, the way you're trying to do now, Michael. And I let him because, for me, it was like Kerry all over again, and I didn't want to go through that. With Kerry, when our time together was coming to an end he desperately wanted to say so many things to me, to make sure that I would be taken care of. That was important to him and I know it was his biggest worry, yet I would never let him talk about it because I was so adamant about avoiding the obvious, *that my husband was dying*. I lived in the delusion that if I didn't talk about it, that would somehow change things. Like you're doing, I think. So in the end, when Kerry and I most needed to talk, to say everything we'd thought we would have a lifetime to say, I couldn't do it. I wasted so much time, Michael. Time I'll never get back. Things I'll never get to say to the man I loved so dearly. Things I'll never get to hear him say to me. Then Cameron…I knew he wasn't well, but I didn't push it, even though he was in denial. For me, it was safer. And, trust me, I know denial. But when I should have been talking to him…" She paused, blinking back the inevitable tears.

"It was a doomed relationship before that, and one that was just hanging on by a fraying thread when his diagnosis of leukemia was finally made. So there I was, engaged to marry a man I knew I'd never walk down the aisle with and trying hard to be the support he needed in a difficult time for him. Avoidance is such a hurtful, terrible thing to do to yourself, or to someone you care about. We became so…es-tranged, because there were so many things that needed saying. Honest feelings I just couldn't face up to, and Cameron needed that honesty from me, especially when he was so sick, but I was holding back again.

"It was bad for both of us. Yet I couldn't leave him, even though I was on the verge of it when his leukemia hit, and I truly believe that the strains we were putting our relationship through at the time made his condition worse. Or, at least, caused him undue stress he didn't deserve, and which he didn't need, going into chemotherapy. But I stood by, and it was horrible for both of us because I think we both knew that we would have already ended the relationship if not for his illness.

"But the thing was, Cameron never knew about Kerry. Cameron was my rebound love after Kerry died and all Cameron ever knew was that I'd been married before. I never told him more than that and he never asked. Then one day, when Cameron was having a particularly bad bout from his chemo, I told him about an herbal tea that had always settled Kerry's stomach when he had been going through the same thing. It just slipped out. I hadn't meant it to, but there it was."

"And that's when you ended your relationship to Cameron?" he asked.

She shook her head. "That's when he ended his relationship with me. He said I should have told him, and he was right. And I let him down, Michael, just like I did Kerry. I avoided too much, and Cameron sent me away at a time he needed someone to be with him. I could have stayed as a friend, but we were past that point."

"Twice, Sarah… I don't know what to say."

"There's nothing to say. Life doesn't come with guarantees, does it? I was angry and bitter both times, but mostly hurt. It was easier to run away than face up to so many bad decisions. So I ran."

"But both of them made their choices too, Sarah. I don't want to speak ill of your husband, but it was his choice to *let* you avoid the things you didn't want to face. He could have insisted on having those talks you never had, to say those things that never got said. But I have an idea that his choice was to protect you from them because you were so afraid of them, the way it was Cameron's choice to ignore his symptoms even when you were telling him to get help."

"But if I'd been stronger… I wasn't strong enough to help them through the way they needed to be helped. *And that's the point.* My inadequacies are the reason I quit medicine. I was there for them, but not enough, and not in the right way. Which is the same thing as failing them."

"It's not about your strength, Sarah. You are strong. I've seen that. What you've gone through, twice, are the kinds of things no one is ever prepared to deal with, and sometimes it's just a matter of getting through the best way you can. You can't keep condemning yourself for that."

"But it wasn't supposed to be about me. Not with Kerry, not with Cameron. Cameron said that if he'd known what I'd gone through with Kerry he'd have let me go long before he did. I think he knew that the friction we already had between us worsened his condition. I tried, Michael, but it wasn't right between us. But I didn't want him to…"

"To die alone?" he asked, his voice tender. "The way you didn't want me to die alone?"

Finally, the tears broke, and she took an angry swipe at them. "People were hateful after Cameron broke it off. They accused me of terrible things, even though Cameron defended me and told everyone that he was the one to leave me. But no one believed that. They simply assumed that I couldn't take it. Or didn't want to." She ducked her head as Michael walked down the stairs then straight over to her and pulled her into his arms. "Which is why I came here today. I have a terrible history of not saying the right things, or not saying anything at all, and I can't do that again, Michael. Not with you."

"And this time you didn't run, even though that's what I've been trying to force, telling you to leave me alone."

She nodded, as the tears streaking down her face blotted against his sweater. "I let down the people I love. I don't mean

to, but that's how it works out. How can I be a good doctor
when I can't even do what I need to do for the people I love?
Twice, Michael. I've failed twice. I missed the obvious, let
myself be talked out of something I knew, couldn't bring
myself to say or hear the right words… Those are all horrible
traits in a doctor. When I took my oath I vowed to do my best,
and that includes seeing everything, insisting when the
patient is protesting, saying what needs to be said and, most
of all, listening. Without the ability to do those, I can't be a
doctor."

"So why are you here now, Sarah?"

"Because I couldn't fail you, Michael. I fell in love with
you and I had to tell you. I know you heard me say it when
you were sick, but I wanted you to hear it when you were
well. I thought that maybe, if you loved me like you said you
did, hearing it from me again would help you get through
whatever it is you're going through. Maybe it would give you
something to hold onto. As simple as that. I used to go around
thinking there was always enough time, but there's not. And
I don't want to make any mistakes with you. Not like I've
done with everybody else. So, I do love you, and that's why
I'm here." She felt his body go rigid against hers. "I know
you have feelings for me, but if the reason you've been re-
sisting me is because of your leg…"

He pulled away from her, but not to retreat up the stairs.
like she feared that he might. Instead, he marched to the
other side of the room, to the liquor cabinet, where he pulled
out a bottle of something she thought to be Scotch.

"I don't know if we can work it out between us," she continued, as he poured a shot in a small glass, then drank it
straight down. "But at least I've come here to try. It wasn't
easy, Michael. I'd promised myself I'd never get involved
again, because that only led to being let down, or to a broken
heart. But I'm not one of those people who denies her
feelings. I didn't want to fall in love with anybody, but I did

fall in love with you. That's why this is so hard for me, because I know how much you didn't want to fall in love with me. But I think you did, Michael. I *know* you did."

He turned around to face her. "I'm glad you've been able to work through your problems, Sarah. I'm sure that in time you'll return to medicine, find yourself a man who deserves you, settle down and have yourself a nice life. But not with me." He started to pour himself another drink, which was uncharacteristic of him. It was an obvious sign she couldn't miss, and he wasn't going to put her off the way Cameron had. She was heart and soul in love with the man who'd given her back the life she'd always loved, and now it was her turn to find a way to give him back his life. But if his disability wasn't the cause of this, what was?

"I've never asked because I figured that if you wanted me to know, you'd tell me. But how did you lose your leg, Michael? What happened?"

"I told you it's not connected to my leg!" he snapped.

"And if you've convinced yourself of that, you're lying to yourself because even if your leg isn't the whole cause of what you're suffering, it plays a part."

"Oh, that's right. This is where you get to be insistent with me, the way you couldn't be with Cameron. Except with me it isn't going to work." He stared at his second drink for a moment before he drank it down. "So you can go now, Sarah."

"Was it something stupid you did to yourself? Motorcycle accident? Some other kind of sport-related injury?" She hated this, but she wasn't ready to give up on Michael yet, not when he was so close to giving up on himself. "Car wreck? Cancer? Diabetic complication?"

"Go away," he snapped, brushing his hand through his hair.

"I read about a climber who got his arm caught by a rock and had to do a self-amputation. Were you a climber? Maybe it was severe frostbite? Tell me, Michael. Tell me what happened."

"It's nobody's business what happened." He picked up the Scotch bottle for a third go at it, studied the bottle with pure revulsion on his face, then hurled the mostly full bottle at the wall. It crashed with a vengeance, sending glass shards everywhere while the butterscotch-colored alcohol ran down the wood panels. "Just go away Sarah," he said, this time the anger all drained from his voice. "There's nothing here for you."

"An industrial accident?" she asked. "Something alcohol-related? Some kind of infection? A compound fracture that wouldn't heal?"

He sucked in a deep, rapid breath and forced it out just as quickly. "A landmine. I stepped on a damned landmine and it exploded. So are you happy now that you know? Happy enough to get the hell away from me?"

Dear God, she hadn't even been close. "You were in the military?" That surprised her, yet in a way it didn't, as exact as he was about his actions, about the way he practiced his medicine. He did have that military precision about him, didn't he?

"That's right. I was military. It was all I ever wanted—to be a doctor in a military hospital like my father had been. From battlefield surgeon to cruise-ship doctor all because I…" He broke off, shook his head and headed for the stairs again, but on the way Sarah caught him by the arm, and wouldn't let go.

"Tell me the rest of it, Michael."

"What makes you think there's more to tell? I got sloppy. Walked somewhere I shouldn't have." With his hand, he made a sweeping gesture toward his leg. "And this is what I got for it. Are you satisfied now?" He shook her off, but she grabbed hold of his arm again, this time fighting to hang on.

"I know what Kerry saw when he looked in the mirror,

Michael. I know what broke his heart. But what do you see when *you* look in the mirror? What breaks your heart?"

"What breaks my heart is a self-centered, selfish bastard who couldn't be bothered to stand by his men. That's what I see." He spun away from her and marched up the stairs, but by the time he was at the top, she was right behind him.

"You forced me to take a good, hard look at myself, Michael. That's how I'm able to come to you now. In the note you left me, when you said that I needed to live my life for myself, that meant something to me because I really haven't ever done that. At least, not much in the past years. When I thought about it, I realized what that life was. My medical practice. *And you*. That's the life I want to live for myself."

"Well, good for you, Sarah. Except you can only have half of that."

"But I don't want half of it."

"Then call me selfish for cheating you out of everything you want, because that's what I am. Selfish. This is all about me, not you."

"You're not selfish, Michael. I've seen that. You care so deeply for people."

"Yeah, like I cared so much that I sent my two medics out while I stayed back and took a nap. Sent them out to die while I went to bed, and it got them killed."

"I don't believe that!" she sputtered.

"Believe what? That I could put myself first? That's what I did. We were all tired. All equally tired, but somebody had to go, and it was my decision to make. So I sent two people out who were as tired as I was and they went the wrong damn way. Traveled into an area that hadn't been cleared and got themselves killed doing it. And the hell of it was, it was a non-essential trip. People had to be transported from a first-aid station to the hospital, but they weren't critical. We could have waited. But I issued the order, and even though my men asked to hold back for an hour or two so they could rest, I made them go anyway."

"But you couldn't have known... I mean, you can't predict the outcome in a war zone."

"Maybe you can't, but you up the odds of making it a bad one when you send war-weary troops out into the middle of it."

"So, how did you...?" She pointed to his right leg. "How did that happen?"

"After I heard the explosion, I ran that half mile to get to them...don't even remember it." He paused, shut his eyes, then drew in a ragged breath. "Rather than sticking to the road, which I knew had been de-mined, I veered off to get there faster, and stepped on a landmine. I don't remember anything after that for about a week. And they gave me a damned medal for doing nothing."

No more words. Michael marched into the bedroom and slammed the door shut behind him, leaving Sarah standing alone on the stairs. She didn't know what to say, didn't know what to do. Turning around, she started back down the stairs, but had taken only a few steps when Michael's words came back to her. *Let your heart tell you what to do. Listen, Sarah. It won't let you down.*

She prayed that would be the case as she climbed those stairs again, then pushed open Michael's bedroom door. "I could say something trite like accidents happen, or there was no way you could have known what would happen, but I won't because your pain goes too deep for that. But what I will say, Michael, is that what happened to you changed you to the very core. I'm not sure you were ever as bad as you think. We all change, get touched by the world in ways we didn't know we could. Maybe you were selfish, staying behind to take a nap. I don't think you ever could be selfish, but I wasn't there so I really can't say. Or maybe it's more a case of you being too hard on yourself. Whichever it is, the Michael Sloan I know right now isn't the one who existed back then, and the one I know now isn't selfish. He's a caring, generous man who loves medicine, and has the pure heart of the five-year-old who wanted to save those people on the freighter. What counts…*the only thing that counts*…is that you make your life matter for something good."

He laughed bitterly. "I'm damaged goods," he said.

"So am I, but you've made me realize that damage can be repaired, or at the very least turned into something better. I know the guilt you're feeling over losing your men…your friends. God knows, I have had my share of loss. But as doctors we know better than most that there are some things we just can't control. That includes death. Even though I know I let Kerry down, I don't think he ever thought I did. Cameron, too. And your men…if they knew you the way I've come to, I don't believe they would have thought you were letting them down."

"But it doesn't matter what they thought, does it? I did let them down. However you look at it, I did."

"That's how *you* look at it, Michael. But what I see is a very brave man who would have given his own life to save them." She walked slowly to the large picture window where he was standing. His back was turned to her as she slipped her arms around his waist and laid her head against him. "We're our own harshest judges, aren't we? You blaming yourself, me blaming myself."

"Sometimes we have to be."

"But there's a time to let go. There's got to be because I always wanted to love again, in spite of not believing I really could. You know, that little speck of hope hiding deep down inside. Then I met you, Michael, and the little speck grew, which really scared me because it's so much easier to live within the restrictions we set for ourselves than step outside them. But everything about you made me want to step outside them. The heart has such an amazing capacity for expanding and changing, doesn't it?"

"Maybe it does," he whispered, "but that's not going to change things between us."

She hadn't expected this to be easy, but she wasn't giving up. "No, it's not. I love you, and I know you love me."

"Look, Sarah, regardless of how I might feel about you, I didn't want to meet you. Not yet."

His voice was softening, taking on the gentle qualities she expected from Michael yet still fighting them. But she wasn't going to approach him again. This time he would have to come to her. "And I didn't want to meet you. Maybe not ever. But there's one unavoidable thing we have to face here. *We met, Michael*. And we found each other over and over on that big cruise ship, even when we weren't trying to."

"At the wrong time."

"Or the right time…the time we most needed to meet. And be together."

"But I can't." He finally turned to face her.

"Why not?"

"I was engaged once, and…"

"And she walked out on you after your injury?" It had been a wild guess, but the answer was in his eyes. "Do you really think I'm that shallow?"

"Not shallow. Duty-bound, maybe. But not shallow."

"Believe me, that night in Evangeline's had nothing to do with being duty-bound. And I'd do it again, in a heartbeat." She drew in a steadying breath, still in for the fight. "That's not me, Michael. You know that's not me."

"Maybe I do, but the life I'd planned for myself is gone and there's nothing left in its place. That's where I am, Sarah. In a place where there's nothing. I want to be a doctor. That's never changed, even though I'll never be a military surgeon again. But I don't know how I'm going to work it out, and I don't know where. Until I do, I can't bring someone else into that uncertainty. Can't bring you. You deserve better."

"Even if that someone else wants to be there with you? Because I do, Michael. I don't know where my life is going either, but wherever it goes, the only thing I know for certain is that I want you to be there, in it. I don't even care about the rest of the details. What I want is you, any way I can have you."

"You *are* stubborn. Of course, I knew that the first time I set eyes on you…the way you defied doctor's orders about your hypoglycemia."

"Not so much defied them as adjusted them to suit my needs." She smiled. "The way I'm trying to adjust *you* to suit my needs."

"How can we do this, Sarah?"

"Together. That's the first step, and maybe the only one we should take right now. I think we're good for that much, Michael. One step at a time, one day at a time."

"I do love you, you know. Every time I've said it, I meant it."

"I know," she whispered, on the verge of tears again. She desperately wanted to run into his arms, but she wouldn't. She'd made every move toward him she knew how to make, bared her soul, allowed Michael into places in herself no man had ever touched, but now it was time for him to want her. She'd taken that first step toward him and now it was his turn to take that same step toward her, so she stood her ground, even though it was very difficult. "And I love you, too."

They stared at each other for a moment, with all the longing of two broken hearts in their gazes. Yet Michael didn't go to her, and she wondered if he would. She still did believe she'd let Kerry down when he'd needed her the most, the way she'd also let Cameron down. Both in different ways, yet both with so much pain. Now she was beginning to wonder if Michael thought that she would let him down, too.

Nothing intentional, nothing planned, but an accumulation of all her inadequacies.

Maybe it was time to go. Maybe the character flaw that Michael had convinced her wasn't a flaw really was after all. And he saw that. "I, um…" she began, then stopped. This time she'd said everything. There was nothing remaining and she had no regrets as she'd told him everything in her heart. Drained her soul dry. After that, there was nothing left to do but to go, and leave Michael to figure it out on his own.

She didn't want to leave him because she feared he would be glad she'd taken the easiest way out. Yet she couldn't stay. Not any longer. So, without another word, she turned and walked through the bedroom door, then down the stairs, each and every one of her footsteps leaden. Halfway to the front door she heard the faint click of the bedroom door upstairs, and a large knot caught in her throat. He'd shut her out, and she'd never get back in. Ten more steps and she'd be out of his life for ever.

She'd only taken five of those ten, however, when he called to her. "Sarah, don't go!"

She held her breath, without turning to face him.

"I don't have any answers," he said. "I know you've never let down the people you think you have…"

"And you didn't let down your men."

"But it's going to take more than words to convince either of us, isn't it? Knowing it on the surface and feeling it in the heart are entirely different."

"Survivor's guilt," she said. "Both of us. It happens. The one who doesn't die experiences guilt over it as part of the way they deal with it. I don't know how to get through it, Michael."

"Together," he whispered. "We have to get through it together."

"Together."

"I don't know how it's going to work out, Sarah. The only

thing I do know for certain is that I want you there with me when it does. More than that, I want to be there with you. Can you accept all the other uncertainties that go with it?"

She nodded. She couldn't speak now as tears flooded down her cheeks. But she heard him walk down the stairs and cross over the wooden floor, and by the time he reached her and pulled her into his arms, she was certain of *only* one thing among the many things she still wasn't sure of. She loved Michael Sloan. Nothing else mattered.

Third time *was* the charm. This was where she was meant to be.

"I love you," he whispered. His entire body relaxed as he held her.

So did hers as she clung to him for dear life, happy and contented. Finally, after so long, Sarah had found her life again, and it was with Michael. Only Michael… "I love you, too."

"You should look at this," Sarah said, tossing the medical journal across the bed to Michael. Things were getting better. They moved forward in small steps each day, always together. She still carried her guilt, so did Michael, and with each other's help they were coming to understand the nature of their guilt and help each other through it. It was amazing how much lighter the load was when it was carried by two. In the rough moments they worked through it together. In the good moments it was perfect.

Being married to Michael was everything she'd ever hoped for. And more.

"You read enough medical journals for the two of us," he grumbled, pulling the sheet up over his head. He'd been off duty for the grand total of an hour and he wasn't anywhere near ready to wake up. Especially since he'd had more than his fair share of cruise overeaters come into the hospital the night before—overeaters like Mrs Grimaldi, who'd made a light snack of a pound of shrimp, a lobster, and half a chocolate cake. "But you're going to tell me about it anyway, aren't you?" he groaned.

"It's about a little clinic in a country near Thailand. They're doing remarkable things for victims of landmines and other similar traumas."

That caught his attention, and he finally turned over. "So…"

"So, they're expanding. Opening an amputee clinic specifically for children. Predicting great things, according to the article you don't want to read."

He reached over, trying to grab it away from Sarah, but she held it out of his reach and waved it at him just to taunt him. "If you want it, you're going to have to pay for it," she teased.

"And what kind of payment would the lady like in exchange for a used journal?"

"I think you know what I want," she purred, dropping the magazine on the floor next to the bed. She slid down her pillow just enough so that when Michael came sailing over her to grab the journal, she was able to do a little grabbing of her own. "There's really nothing else to read," she whispered in his ear, as she turned ever so slightly on her side and raised her leg over his hip. "And since I don't have to be on duty for another two hours, I thought…"

He was instantly aroused. She could see it, the way she could see the eagerness in his eyes right now that was there for something other than her. Smiling, she slid on top of him just a bit more. "I do have something to tell you," she said as he let the journal fall back to the floor.

"Right now, I'd rather you *show* me…" Before he'd finished the sentence, Sarah pushed him all the way over on his back, then straddled him. In a flash, he reached up under the T-shirt she always wore to bed, one of his, to find her breasts. "Just like that," he growled, as she wiggled out of the shirt. "That's exactly what I want you to show me."

"I have something even better," she said, leaning over him until her breasts were in his face. He had only started to nibble when she pulled back and thrust a piece of paper at him she'd grabbed off the bedside table.

"It had better be sexy," he warned, giving her an exaggerated scowl.

"Well, not so much sexy as satisfying, I think."

That piqued his curiosity enough that he grabbed the paper. The instant he laid eyes on it, she sucked in a sharp breath and held it.

The words on the paper were brief, and after less than half a minute he turned to look at her. "I…I don't know what to say."

"Yes, for starters. It's everything we want, Michael. Everything we've talked about these past couple of months."

"They want us to run the children's amputee clinic?"

She nodded. "After I saw the posting this morning I e-mailed them, just to enquire about the position, nothing else. While you were still on duty. They e-mailed back within an hour, wanting more details about us, then made the offer a little while after I told them who we are. They said they checked our credentials, thanks to the marvels of modern technology, and if we'd like a job with little pay, long hours, lots of hard work, and more satisfaction than we could imagine…"

"And how long were you going to keep this from me?"

She smiled. "Just long enough to write this…" She handed him another piece of paper from the bedside stand. This one was handwritten, from herself to Michael. It was a letter of resignation from her position as ship's doctor, giving him two weeks' notice. The reason stated was that she was going to work with her husband in a little clinic near Thailand. "I think Martha will probably come along as my nurse, if I ask her," she said. "And I'd suggest you ask Ina along as *your* nurse, if you know what's good for you."

A sexy grin slid to his lips. "You really think you know me so well that you can anticipate my decision, don't you?" Both letters in his hand fluttered to the floor as he rolled over to face her. "Don't you?"

Laughing, Sarah snaked her hand around Michael's neck. "I do. And just to prove it, I'm making another decision right now that you're going to love."

"Anything you want to tell me about?"

She pulled his face toward hers. "I'd rather show you."

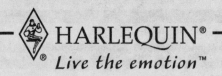

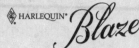

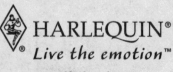

HARLEQUIN®

>*American* ★ *Romance*®

Invites *you* to experience lively, heartwarming all-American romances

Every month, we bring you four strong, sexy men, and four women who know what they want—and go all out to get it.

From small towns to big cities, experience a sense of adventure, romance and family spirit—the all-American way!

>*American* ★ *Romance*®

Love, Home & Happiness

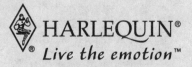
HARLEQUIN®
Live the emotion™

HARLEQUIN®
INTRIGUE®

BREATHTAKING ROMANTIC SUSPENSE

Shared dangers and passions lead to electrifying romance and heart-stopping suspense!

Every month, you'll meet six new heroes who are guaranteed to make your spine tingle and your pulse pound. With them you'll enter into the exciting world of Harlequin Intrigue— where your life is on the line and so is your heart!

THAT'S INTRIGUE—
ROMANTIC SUSPENSE
AT ITS BEST!

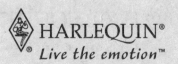

HARLEQUIN®
Live the emotion™

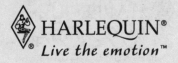

HARLEQUIN®
Presents®

**The world's bestselling romance series...
The series that brings you your favorite authors,
month after month:**

Helen Bianchin...Emma Darcy
Lynne Graham...Penny Jordan
Miranda Lee...Sandra Marton
Anne Mather...Carole Mortimer
Melanie Milburne...Michelle Reid

and many more talented authors!

Wealthy, powerful, gorgeous men...
Women who have feelings just like your own...
The stories you love, set in exotic, glamorous locations...

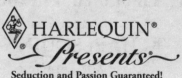

HARLEQUIN®
Presents®

Seduction and Passion Guaranteed!

www.eHarlequin.com

Harlequin® Historical
Historical Romantic Adventure!

Imagine a time of chivalrous knights and unconventional ladies, roguish rakes and impetuous heiresses, rugged cowboys and spirited frontierswomen— these rich and vivid tales will capture your imagination!

Harlequin Historical . . . they're too good to miss!